THE
BURNING
SOUL

BOOKS BY DAWN MERRIMAN

THE
BURNING
SOUL

DAWN MERRIMAN

SECOND SKY

Published by Second Sky in 2025

An imprint of Storyfire Ltd.
Carmelite House
50 Victoria Embankment
London EC4Y 0DZ

www.secondskybooks.com

The authorised representative in the EEA is Hachette Ireland
8 Castlecourt Centre
Dublin 15 D15 XTP3
Ireland
(email: info@hbgi.ie)

ISBN: 978-1-83618-992-3
eBook ISBN: 978-1-83618-991-6

This book is dedicated to my husband, Kevin.
I could not write these stories without you.

ONE

RYLAN FLYNN

Keaton's bedroom door hangs open, boxes tossed aside in the hall.

"Did I do good?" the little girl ghost, Elsa, asks. "I just realized I can move things."

My mouth refuses to move, my jaw slack with shock.

"What's wrong?" the ghost of my mom asks. "You look terrified."

I slowly turn. "What have you done?" I ask in a low whisper. "I've kept that thing locked in here for years."

Elsa looks like she might cry, her blue eyes shining. "I-I... The man inside begged me. He said he got stuck in there and wanted out." She sniffles. "I didn't see a man, though. It was something else."

"It's not a man," I say. I lean through the doorway, looking inside the dim room. The thing I've kept in here is nowhere to be seen. "It must have gotten out."

"Rylan, what are you talking about? What's wrong?" Mom asks with a mixture of annoyance and concern.

Something crashes from another room. "I'll show you," I say and lead them down the hall.

"Is it dangerous?" Elsa asks, huddling behind Mom.

"You're ghosts, I don't think it can hurt you," I say, peeking around the corner to see into the dining room. Unfortunately, there are too many boxes and things in the way.

"Rylan, you're scaring us," Mom says.

Another crash, this one from the kitchen, the unmistakable sound of breaking plates.

The thing laughs.

Elsa covers her ears. "I don't like that laughter. It's bad."

"The thing is bad," I say. "And it's growing stronger. That's probably why you can hear it now."

I inch around the corner, crouching behind the piles. In the hoard I see a tall statue of a woman with a pitcher and grab it as a weapon.

"What are you going to do?" Mom whispers.

The laughing and breaking plates suddenly stop.

"Ryyyylannn," it calls. "Come play with me."

Hearing it call my name makes my skin crawl, but I take another step. On my tiptoes, I look over the top of a pile.

It perches on my kitchen bar, uglier than I remember. The puppet is the size of a small child, but so much worse. A marionette of a jester paces on my counter, laughing and calling my name.

He sees me and the eyes blink, dark pools in the blue stars painted on his jester's face. The horrible mouth, painted red and too big, opens.

"About time you faced me," he hisses.

"I'm not afraid of you," I say, stepping around the boxes. The banging of my heart belies my words.

He raises an arm, the strings above his head pulled by an invisible hand. The movement makes the bells on the ends of his hat jingle. "What about them? I bet the little girl will be afraid."

I glance behind me in question.

"I hear him, but I can't see anything. Where is it?" Elsa asks, trying to see over the pile in front of us.

"You don't want to see," Mom says, trying to shield her. "It's horrible."

Now that he has my attention, he throws his hands up in the air and screams. A bright green light emanates around him. "Now that I'm free, I can finally be whole." The light grows brighter, so intense it hurts my eyes. The puppet screams and electric energy makes the hair on the back of my neck tickle.

Elsa and Mom both gasp.

"What an awful toy," Elsa says.

"It's no longer a toy," I say, lifting the statue, ready to swing if it comes at us.

The jester puppet stops screaming.

"What do you want?" I ask, faking bravery. The green light has faded, but the energy in the room feels evil.

"I'll show you in time," the jester says. He jumps from the counter and rushes toward the patio door. With a last shriek, he crashes through the glass and out into the night.

"Stop!" I shout and run to the door. "We can't let him loose." I pull the door open and step over the broken glass. Searching left and right, I hope to see him, but he's disappeared into the dark of Ashby.

Mom and Elsa join me on the back patio. "Where would that horrible thing go?" Mom asks.

My heart sinks in despair. "I have no idea, but he's dangerous. That's why I had him locked in that room."

"I'm so sorry," Elsa says, sniffling. "I didn't know."

"How long has that monster been locked in Keaton's room? How did I not know?"

I rub my arms, chilled by the night air despite my leather jacket. "Let's go inside and I'll explain." I pull the remains of the patio door closed.

"That hole is going to let the cold in," Mom says. "Plus, what if it comes back?"

"Good point." I slide a stack of boxes in front of the hole, although I don't think the boxes will hold it anymore. He's grown stronger now that he's escaped.

Mom and Elsa stare at me with identical expressions of fear and question.

"First, I need a drink. This has been a long, long night."

I step around the broken plates on my kitchen floor and find the makings of a vodka tonic buried in a cabinet. I mix the drink in silence, then take a long swallow. Only then do I turn to face the questions hanging in the air.

"It all started years ago when I first started seeing ghosts. Keaton was still here then. Sometimes, I would see a moving shadow in his room when I'd walk by or hear a soft, evil laugh. I did my best to ignore it and I never went into that room."

"Was it the puppet you were seeing?" Mom asks. "I remember when Keaton brought that marionette home. He said he found it at the dump. I didn't like it from the start."

"I think he brought some evil spirit home in the puppet." I take another long drink, the vodka warming my belly. "That's how things were for a long time. I had a feeling something was wrong in there but wasn't sure what to do. Keaton moved out and I just closed his door. Then I moved out and I pretty much forgot about it."

"I rarely went in there, either. I left it just as he had it when he moved out," Mom says wistfully.

"Complete with the puppet on the shelf," I continue. "Except once I moved back in, things changed. The puppet would make noises. It would laugh and howl and I'd hear it moving around sometimes. That's when I decided I had to keep it locked up."

"How did you keep it in the room? It crashed through the patio door, why didn't it just go through the window?" Elsa asks.

"Let me show you."

I lead them to Keaton's room and turn on the light.

"Oh my," Mom says.

"Wow," Elsa says.

The walls are covered in crosses of all sizes. Even the window has three. On the back of the door is a large one. "I took down all Keaton's stuff and replaced it with crosses," I explain. "I hoped it would keep the evil inside. And it worked."

None of us want to step into the creepy room. We just look in from the hall.

"Until I let him out," Elsa says miserably.

"Why could Elsa hear him and I couldn't?" Mom asks. "I can't believe I didn't know he was in here."

"I don't know. Maybe because children are more in tune with things like that. No one has been able to hear him except me. Until now."

Mom turns away from the cross-covered room. "What do we do now? That thing is running through town. If we can see it and hear it, does that mean everyone else can too?"

"I imagine so."

"You need to call Ford and tell him."

"I don't want to do that," I hedge.

"Your little breakup won't last. That man loves you. Besides, if there's an evil possessed marionette wreaking havoc on Ashby, he needs to know."

"Maybe it didn't go far," I say half-heartedly, heading back to the kitchen and my drink, not sure what to do. Mom's right, I should tell Ford, but what am I supposed to say? He doesn't even want to talk to me right now, let alone hear this crazy story.

I down the rest of my drink wishing it would solve my problem. Mom and Elsa watch me intently, like I have the answers.

"What are you going to do?" Elsa asks.

I sit the empty glass next to several others by the sink. "I have no idea."

I wish Ford was with me. I wish Mom was alive and could hug my problems away like she did when I was young. The weight of my responsibilities pushes on my mind. I straighten my shoulders and run a hand through my tangled hair.

"We'll help you," Elsa says innocently.

"Yeah. You're not alone in this," Mom adds.

This makes me smile and warms my heart.

"I appreciate that," I say.

"Look, I can help pick up the broken plates," Elsa says, picking up a shard.

"I don't know what I'd do without you guys," I say. I don't want to think about the day they cross over. I have enough problems for one night.

"Maybe you should go lie down for a while," Mom says. "I don't know what you can do tonight and it's way past midnight."

I want to argue with her, but when I open my mouth, a huge yawn takes over my face. "I should go look for the puppet," I say.

"In the morning. You don't even know where to start looking or what to do if you find him. Things will look different in the light of day," Mom says.

I listen to my mother and go to my room, kick off my sneakers and climb into bed. "I should"s and "I need to"s fill my mind, but I curl onto my side anyway. Maybe Mom is right and things will look better when the sun comes up.

Although I'm exhausted, sleep will not come. I stare at my ceiling for a long time, worrying, wondering.

I lie like this for a long time, until the sound of sirens scream through the night.

TWO

RYLAN FLYNN

I fly out of bed and grab my shoes, not sure where I'm going, but sure the puppet has something to do with the sirens.

All my fault. All my fault.

I hurry down the hall to the kitchen where I find Mom and Elsa again picking up the broken plates.

"Look, we're helping," Elsa says with pride as she drops a shard into the trash. "I'm getting good at moving things."

"I even picked one up," Mom says. She looks up from the trash and freezes when she sees my face. "What's wrong?"

"There's sirens outside. That has to be related to the puppet out there."

She cocks her head to listen. "Oh, there *are* sirens. I hadn't noticed."

I look out the window to the backyard. The sky is glowing to the north.

I grab my car keys and head out the broken patio door and into the yard.

"Rylan, where are you going?" Mom calls as I hurry around the house toward my old Cadillac.

"I want to check out the fire. I might be able to help."

"You're not a firefighter. What could you possibly do?" Mom says reasonably.

I stop in the front yard. She's right. What can I do?

"I don't know, but I feel like I need to go."

"That thing is out there," Elsa says. "It might hurt you."

"Even more reason for me to go. If that marionette is running around Ashby, I need to find it."

"Roland," Mom says.

I look at her with curiosity. "Roland? What are you talking about?"

"The puppet's name is Roland. That's what Keaton used to call it."

"Whatever its name, I need to find it and destroy it." I jog across the yard to my car.

"Can we come?" Elsa asks.

"No. I don't want to have to worry about you two and the Roland puppet."

"But who's going to worry about you?" Mom asks. "It can't be safe."

"You'll worry enough for the both of us," I say, climbing into the car. Mom and Elsa stand in the front yard and watch as I drive away. Elsa raises her hand and waves. I give her a wave back and drive into the night, following the glow in the sky toward the fire.

As I drive the few blocks, I scan the sidewalks and between the houses. I hope to find Roland but also hope not to find him. The thought of the thing I so carefully had locked away for the last two years terrifies me. What is he capable of? If Mom and Elsa can both now hear him, does that mean everyone can? Does that mean everyone is in danger?

My back begins to tingle as I turn a corner near the blaze. The tingle grows more insistent when I see the fire trucks in front of the house. I park down the block, staying out of the way, but drawn to the flames. A crowd has grown behind the trucks. I join the throng of onlookers and watch the fire department do their work, the tingle in my back growing stronger.

Flames climb out of one upper window and thick smoke fills the air, but the busy firefighters have the blaze mostly under control. The front yard is full of activity and hoses. The spinning lights of the trucks fill the night.

Amid all the chaos, I see her.

A woman stands near the house, too close to the flames to be safe. She doesn't seem to notice the heat. Dressed in pajama pants and an overly large, bright pink Hello Kitty T-shirt, she obviously doesn't belong in the thick of things.

I want to yell to her, but I'm conscious of the crowd around me. All I can do is watch the woman. She seems totally confused and has both her hands in her bright pink pixie-cut hair, pulling at the short strands in agitation.

One of the firefighters brushes past her, almost through her.

"Hey, watch it!" she shouts, turning. From this angle, I can see her lip is pierced in two places, the rings glinting in the fire-light. She looks from the firefighter to the gathered crowd. I raise my hand, trying to get her attention without anyone noticing.

She sees me.

I push out of the crowd, motioning inconspicuously for her to follow. I stop down the block and am pleased to see she follows.

"What's going on?" the pink-haired woman asks when she joins me.

I look down so no one notices me talking. "That's what I was going to ask you. Do you know why you're here?"

"I don't even know how I got here. I was in my apartment and now I'm at this fire."

"How long have you been here?"

"Not long, I think. Just before the fire department arrived." She looks back toward the house. "I don't understand. This is all so strange." She runs a hand through her short hair again, making it stick up.

I look her over for obvious signs of injury, a cause for her death. I don't see blood or gunshots. There's a faint line around her neck that may be a ligature mark. Hard to tell in the firelight.

"I know this is hard. Let's start at the beginning. What's your name?"

"My name is Dixie." She looks down at her hands, the fingers full of rings. "I feel weird."

Behind her the familiar light to the other side opens. A rectangle of lovely white.

"Dixie, you need to listen to me," I say, growing desperate and talking fast. "You have died and are about to cross over to the other side." She sees me looking behind her and turns.

"What's that?" she asks in awe.

"It's the doorway. Before you go, what happened? Do you remember anything from before you came to this house?"

Dixie looks from the light to me then back. "I don't know. I don't know." She pulls at the hem of her pink T-shirt. "Is it going to hurt?"

"No, it's beautiful there. You will be safe."

She reaches a hand to the light and her face softens. "It is beautiful." She takes a step toward the door.

I panic she will go before I can find out what happened.

"Wait, tell me what you know. Who did this to you?" I point to her neck.

"I'm coming," she calls into the light and steps. In a flash, she's gone and I'm alone on the sidewalk.

I sigh heavily. I don't know much more than I did five minutes ago, except that Dixie is dead and probably recently. So recently she didn't even know. I wish I could have helped her more, could have explained.

She's beyond explanations now. Heaven has her safe and sound.

I turn back around to face the fire. A few steps away, a dark shape I would recognize anywhere stands on the sidewalk.

Ford Pierce.

My life-long love, recent boyfriend and, as of a few hours ago, my ex.

"Rylan, it's the middle of the night, what are you doing here?" he asks with a mix of exasperation and concern.

"I—" I don't know how to explain why I was drawn here. "I saw the flames from my house, so I came."

"Putting yourself where you don't need to be again," he says, his tone hard.

I push my long brown hair behind my shoulder and lift my chin. "Good thing I did."

"Why's that?"

"I think there's a body in that fire." I glance toward the house, the fire mostly contained now. The flames from the upper window now gone.

In the dim light, I see his eyes widen. "Why do you say that?"

"Because I just talked to her. Am I right? Is that why you're here? Fires are not your business normally."

"What did she say?" He gets right to business.

"Why should I tell you? I'm just here where I don't need to be, remember?"

He blows air in exasperation. "Please," he says, strained.

"I only know her first name, Dixie. She didn't even know she was dead yet or what happened. She said she was at her apartment, then she was here. She looked like she might have been strangled with a ligature of some sort. She had a faint mark on her neck."

He just stares at me, his eyes softening. "You got all that? Where is she now?"

"She crossed right before you walked over here."

He nods thoughtfully. "All I know is that the firefighters found a body in the house, so they called me in. Standard procedure." He rubs his stubbled chin, thinking. "You're telling me it's a murder?"

"I'm just telling you what Dixie said and what I saw. Murder sounds likely."

"Okay, then. That changes things. I'll get this scene sealed and we'll go from there."

"Can I do anything?" I ask before I think.

"You've been a big help," he concedes. "But I have it from here."

"Do you know whose house this is?" I ask.

"Not yet. But we will. Why?"

"That FOR SALE sign in the front yard."

"What about it?"

"That's Jamie and Graham's real estate division. They flip the houses and sell them under that business, Rock Solid Real Estate."

THREE
FORD PIERCE

My heart sinks when Rylan tells me that our friend Jamie Blake and her business partner Graham own the burning house with a possible murder victim inside. When I got the call earlier about a body in a fire, I had expected an open and shut case. Fire deaths are unfortunately all too common.

A murder victim in the house of a friend is not common.

Throw Rylan into the mix and you have yourself a mess.

My neck begins to ache.

"You're sure this is Jamie and Graham's real estate company?" I ask Rylan.

Her eyes flash in the fading fire light. "Rock is Graham's last name."

I rub at the ache in my neck. "Okay. Can you do me a favor? Can you just stay out of it? Can you just go home?"

Now her eyes narrow. "I'm not in the scene. This sidewalk is public property. I want to see what happens. I might be able to help. Besides, someone needs to tell Jamie."

"Let me handle that."

Her phone is already out and she's scrolling through her contacts.

"You have enough to do. It will be better coming from me," she says, holding the phone to her ear.

The ache in my neck expands to my shoulders. "Do what you want. You will anyway."

I turn my back on Rylan, exasperated.

My detective partner, Tyler Spencer, waits for me on the sidewalk a few paces away. He grins when I join him.

"Rylan's here already? That girl can sniff trouble from a mile away."

"She said she saw the light in the sky and had to come. It gets worse. She saw the ghost of our murder victim. First name Dixie."

The grin disappears from Tyler's face. "Murder victim? I thought this was a house-fire death, not a murder."

"I did too, but Rylan talked to Dixie and is pretty sure she was murdered and brought here from her apartment."

"I don't suppose this Dixie knows who killed her? Would sure make our job easier."

"You know it's never that easy where Rylan is concerned."

We watch as the firefighters begin wrapping up their equipment, the fire now out. I'm conscious of Rylan also watching a few yards away. The awareness makes my skin tingle. I want to go to her, to tell her I'm sorry, to kiss her until she understands. Her recklessness and running into danger are making me crazy with worry. I almost lost her again tonight and that was the last straw. She can't keep risking her life.

I have a feeling that it's a lesson I can't teach her, but I don't have to watch her self-destruct either. It's my job to protect her, not help her get into trouble.

The new fire chief, Aiden Andrews, approaches Tyler and me. "Detectives," he says by way of greeting. "Good to see you." He pulls off his thick gloves and shakes both our hands.

"We understand you found a body," I say.

"Yeah. It's toward the back."

"Can we go see it?" Tyler asks.

"We have the fire out now, but that part of the house is a total loss. Not safe to go in. Honestly, there's not much left to see," Aiden says.

"Do you suspect arson?" I ask.

"I don't want to jump to that conclusion, but the fire burned hot and fast near the body and not so much in the rest of the house. Yeah, arson could be involved. Why do you ask?"

"We have reason to believe the victim was murdered before the fire started," I say.

"Reason to believe? Who says?" Aiden looks over my shoulder. "Oh, I get it."

I turn, knowing what he's looking at. Rylan has crept closer and is listening to us.

"Your girlfriend saw a ghost or something?" Aiden asks with more interest than contempt.

Rylan hears his question and joins us. "I'm not his girlfriend," she says. "And yes, I saw the ghost of your victim."

Aiden looks from Rylan to me then back to her. His eyes do a quick once-over of her body. The momentary look makes my heart beat faster. She looks good in her leather jacket over skinny jeans and those damn Chuck Taylor sneakers on her feet. She always looks good. But Aiden Andrews doesn't need to be smiling at her the way he is now.

"What did you see?" he asks her, genuinely curious.

"A woman with pink hair and lip piercings and lots of rings on her fingers. Her name is Dixie. She said she was in her apartment and then she was here. She didn't even know she was dead."

Aiden looks impressed. "You learned all that?"

"And I saw a possible ligature mark on her neck," Rylan says.

"Huh. Look out, detectives. We may not need you after all," Aiden says. "I heard you were amazing, but I had no idea."

"I'm not that amazing. I just talk to the spirits that need me."

Is that a blush on her cheeks?

"Yes, Rylan is amazing," I say, stepping slightly between them. "Can you show us the body now, please?"

With a last appreciative look at Rylan, Aiden turns to the smoldering remains of the fire. "Your victim is back here," he says.

Although the fire is out now, the scent of smoke and charring is heavy in the air.

And the scent of burned meat.

I try to block that thought from my mind and focus on the job at hand.

"We found her in the kitchen," Aiden says, walking around the house to the back patio. "She's just inside here. Be careful, it's pretty well destroyed, but should hold up." The two-story house is fairly intact, a testament to the firefighters' quick work. This part of the house, though, is blackened and fragile-looking.

"Maybe we shouldn't go in there," Tyler says. "Looks unstable. What if the floor above falls in?"

My thoughts exactly, but judging by Aiden's expression, I'm glad I didn't say it out loud.

"My men have been in there," he points out.

Tyler looks to me for backup. "Let's go in," I say, surprising myself.

The back door is open and the dark inside of the house looms in front of me. Faking bravery, but secretly shaking inside, I cross into the shell of a kitchen. Tyler follows, grumbling.

"She's on the left, there. Against the wall," Aiden says.

I can barely make out the shape of what used to be a body in the ashes and coals. Above us, the house creaks and I fight not to flinch.

"Not much left," Tyler says. "I'm surprised your men recognized it as a body."

"They're good at their jobs," Aiden says.

I squat next to the remains, not sure what I'm looking for. There really isn't much left. If it wasn't for what Rylan told us, I wouldn't be able to tell if it was a man or woman I'm looking at.

I take out my phone flashlight and shine it all over the body. Rings on the fingers flash in the beam.

Tyler makes a sound of appreciation. "Didn't Rylan say something about rings, lots of them?"

"She did," I say, shifting back to standing. "This must be Dixie." I shine the light on what's left of the face and notice that her lip is pierced too.

The ceiling directly to our right begins to crumble and pieces of blackened drywall fall down.

"Maybe we should get out of here," Tyler says. "Before we get crushed." He hurries to the door, me close behind.

The smoky air feels fresh after being inside the house. "We'll have to get her out of there so Marrero can take her to his lab," I say.

"He should be here soon," Tyler says. "He'll want to see her in place."

"You sure the house isn't about to collapse?" I ask Aiden.

"Nothing sure about fire, but it seems to be holding up. We'll probably have to knock it down eventually for safety, but not until you all are done with your investigation."

"Ford." I hear my name being called from the front of the house. I don't have to turn to know who's calling my name.

I'd recognize her voice anywhere.

I walk around the corner to find Rylan with Jamie and Graham.

"Yes?" I ask with exaggerated patience.

"Graham thinks he knows who the victim is."

FOUR

RYLAN FLYNN

Ford looks annoyed when I call to him, but he brightens at the prospect of a lead. He and Tyler hurry across the yard to the sidewalk where I stand with Jamie and Graham. They ran right over when they found out their house had burned down.

"You think you know our victim?" Ford asks Graham without preamble.

"Well," Graham hedges. "I mean. I know a woman named Dixie that has pink hair and wears lots of rings."

"Just like Rylan saw," Tyler says. "How do you know her?"

Graham looks at the sidewalk. "We dated until a few months ago."

Ford and Tyler exchange a look. "You dated our victim?" Ford says with accusation.

"But he didn't hurt her or burn this house down," Jamie jumps in. The detectives ignore her. They smell a suspect.

"I think you need to come down to the station and give a full statement. If you had anything to do with this, we'll get to the bottom of it," Ford says.

"You can't seriously think Graham did this," I say.

Ford's eyes narrow. "Leave the investigation to us," he says, then turns back to Graham. "What's Dixie's last name?"

"Her actual name is Delores Campbell. She's gone by Dixie since she was a girl," Graham says, his voice breaking. "So she's really gone? You're sure it's her in there?"

"The body is wearing many rings and her lip is pierced. Hard to tell more than that. Dental records and DNA will verify, but for the moment we're going with this theory," Ford says.

I'm glad they believed me about what I saw, but I don't like that it led to Graham. "Just because he knows Dixie doesn't mean he killed her," I say.

"Where were you tonight?" Tyler asks, brushing over my comment.

Graham looks like he might throw up. "I was home asleep."

"Alone?" Ford glances at Jamie.

"Yes, I was alone. Just me and my dog."

"We will definitely need to talk to you officially," Ford says. "After we finish up here, we'll take you down to the station."

Tyler leans into Ford. "Marrero is here with the crime techs."

Tyler looks down the sidewalk with anticipation, no doubt looking for the coroner's tech he is sweet on, Michelle. He smiles when he sees her, then feels me watching and schools his face into a somber expression.

"You should probably go," Ford says to me. "Before Marrero sees you here."

"Why does that matter?" Jamie asks.

"The coroner hates me for some reason," I say. I'm in no mood for facing Marrero tonight, but I don't want to leave my friends, especially with what they think Graham is guilty of. I try to make myself small hoping Marrero won't notice me, but it fails. His sharp eyes pin me to the sidewalk.

"Flynn, again?" He shifts his bag from one hand to the other. "Don't you ever go home?"

I open my mouth to retort, but Ford steps between us. "Right over here." He ushers the coroner toward the crime scene.

"You have to help me," Graham says as Ford, Tyler and Marrero walk away. "You know I didn't have anything to do with this." He takes off his glasses and nervously wipes them on his shirt.

"Of course you didn't," Jamie says. "That's crazy."

"They're just doing what they have to. They'll talk to you and realize you're innocent and then let you go." I think of Aunt Val and when they didn't believe her either. That was different, they had blood evidence that was planted. Graham just has coincidences against him.

Graham doesn't look relieved by my assurances.

"Don't worry," Jamie says, rubbing his shoulder. "You didn't do anything to Dixie, so you will be fine."

He looks up to the sky, blinks back tears. "I can't believe someone would hurt her. I know she was my ex, but she was a good person. Just not the person for me."

"Do you have any ideas who might want to hurt her? Anyone that she had issues with or a fight?" I ask.

"Not that I know of. I haven't talked to her in a few months. She got into it with one of the other stylists at the salon she worked at, but nothing that might lead to murder."

"You never know what will lead to murder. What happened at the salon?"

"She worked with a woman named Rebecca. At first, they got along pretty well, but that turned once I started visiting Dixie for lunch. Rebecca got a little friendly with me. Nothing big or anything that I even noticed, but Dixie got mad about it."

"Mad how?" I ask.

"I wasn't there, but I guess Dixie confronted Rebecca about

it. She told me that they had words. I didn't think too much about it at the time. Dixie could be a bit hot-headed sometimes. That's actually one of the reasons I broke up with her. Too much drama."

"Enough drama to lead to this?" I ask.

"I didn't think so, but here we are," he says miserably. "Besides, it was just that one time they got into it. I think they became friends after that."

"And you broke up," Jamie adds. "Why would it matter now?"

"I agree it's a weak reason, but is there anyone else? Anyone at all? Ford will ask you this too, so better you're prepared beforehand."

"He thinks I did this," Graham says.

"He'll follow where the facts lead. We know this wasn't you, so let's help him figure out who it was. Does Dixie have any other exes that might be mad at her or even mad at you?"

"I really don't know. We only dated a few months and that was over a few months ago. It's not like I know her whole life story," Graham says.

"What about family? Is she from around here?"

"She grew up here, but her only real relative is her sister in Lafayette. Someone will have to tell her about this." His voice crackles a bit, and he swallows hard and rubs at his beard.

"It will be okay," Jamie says, rubbing his arm.

"Will it? Dixie is dead and I'm the prime suspect."

We stand in sad silence for a few minutes, watching the fire-fighters and police and crime scene techs do their jobs. The whole scene feels surreal. It's the middle of the night; the neighborhood should be sleeping. Instead, it's a hot bed of activity.

Out of the corner of my eye, I see a movement in the back-yard of the house next door. At first, I think it's a child, based on the size. Then I recognize the hat with points hanging down.

Roland the marionette is watching the action too.

I freeze, not sure what to do. Until tonight, no one knew the possessed toy existed. Now it's out in the open. I don't know what it wants, but it's something bad. The thing has exuded evil that has just grown in power.

Should I tell them about Roland or pretend I don't see him? Will they even believe me?

They've been through enough tonight; they don't need to know about a possessed puppet that might have just burned their house down and killed their friend.

"I, uh, I will be right back," I say, stepping into the grass of the neighbor's house.

"Where are you going?" Jamie asks.

"I need to check something. Stay here." I make my way around the house to the backyard, my eyes peeled for the puppet. The backyard is dark, and I have no idea what I'll do if I find Roland. I have half an idea of grabbing him by the strings and taking him home to lock him up again.

First, I have to find him.

A shape scurries across the yard toward a shed, making me jump.

"Roland?" I call after him, jogging toward the shed.

He disappears around the small building.

His laughter echoes across the yard and down the alley, making my blood turn cold.

FIVE

FORD PIERCE

Laughter floats across the yard to where I stand with Tyler.

"That's not appropriate for a crime scene," I say, looking over my shoulder to the neighboring yard. It's drenched in shadows, but the laughter is definitely coming from there.

"What isn't?" Tyler asks, looking away suddenly from the tech he was watching.

"The laughter." It suddenly stops.

"I don't hear anything?" he says absently.

"It stopped." I shrug although I'm a little creeped out by the sound, and turn back to watching Marrero's team move the body from the burned house.

The coroner pulls off his gloves. "The fire destroyed most of the body. Based on the jewelry and the general size and shape, I would say it's a woman. I will know more when we get back to the lab."

I don't tell him we already know it's a woman and what her name is. He won't want to hear about information from Rylan.

The laughter starts again. It's a high-pitched, horrible sound.

"What is that?" I ask, turning toward the neighbor's backyard again. Why would someone be out in the middle of the night laughing like that?

Marrero looks annoyed. Tyler looks concerned. "What is that?" he asks.

"Maybe you should ask your girlfriend to keep it down," Marrero says.

Rylan is now in the neighbor's yard, lurking around a shed near the alley.

"Excuse me," I say.

With a sinking feeling, I stride over to her.

Rylan comes around the corner of the shed looking to the roof.

"What's going on over here?" I ask, harsher than I intended.

Rylan jumps, so intent on her searching of the shed she hadn't noticed me.

"Uh, um, I'm not doing anything," she stammers.

"You're a terrible liar. Besides, I already heard the kid laughing. Is he back here?"

"I don't know." She rises on tiptoe to see the roof better.

"You can't just go roaming around in a stranger's backyard," I admonish.

"I'm looking for something."

"In the neighbor's shed? What was that laughing?"

Rylan pulls her leather jacket closer around her and looks at the ground. "I don't know where to start," she says.

"How about at the beginning?" I say, losing patience.

"Do you remember that creepy marionette puppet that Keaton had?" she asks out of the blue.

"The one we found at the dump way back in high school?" I have no idea where this is going, but I play along.

"Well, short story is the puppet is possessed by an evil spirit. I've kept it locked in Keaton's room, but it's escaped. I just saw it in this yard, but it's gotten away."

I just blink at her for several stunned moments. I can hardly believe her, but I know she's telling the truth.

"A possessed marionette?" I ask, rubbing my chin. "At my crime scene?"

"He left now, I think," Rylan says. "He ran around this shed and now I can't find him."

My mind swirls with questions, but I have to focus on my job at the moment. "If it's gone, then we need to get out of this yard." I lead her back toward the sidewalk where Jamie and Graham are waiting, leaning on Rylan's car.

"I don't want to leave," Rylan protests as I knew she would. "I want to help."

"Go catch that puppet. That would be a big help. Do you think it's dangerous?"

"If I thought it was safe, I wouldn't have kept it locked in Keaton's room for all this time."

"How did it get out?" I ask.

Rylan looks away quickly. "I don't want to talk about it."

I know she's hiding something, but I need to get back to work and the investigation. A short way down the block, they're loading the body into the coroner's van.

"We will talk about this, but I can't right now," I say. "If you see the puppet again, let me know. We can't have it causing trouble around town." I can't believe I'm saying these words. Bad enough we have a murderer and arsonist in town. Now I have to contend with a possessed toy that laughs like a demon.

"I think it might be connected to this fire and murder," she says.

My stomach sinks. I was afraid of that.

SIX

RYLAN FLYNN

I watch Ford walk away from me again, my heart breaking a little bit. I'm surprised he took the news about Roland as well as he did. We've been through some crazy paranormal stuff. Darby the possessed bear wasn't evil. This is a bit over the top, even for my life.

It just makes me love Ford more.

"What were you doing back there?" Jamie asks when I rejoin them by my car.

"Just checking something out." I wave her concerns away. I'm not ready to tell them about Roland yet. I need to have a plan to stop him before I tell too many people. Is Roland like Darby the teddy bear was? Does he have a ghost inside him? That ghost is not nice like Elsa is, I'm sure of it. And it's much stronger now that it's loose. Even Ford can hear it.

"Were you laughing? We heard something strange," Jamie says.

I look away, not sure how to answer. "I'm not sure what that was."

We watch as they wrap up the scene, my mind racing with scenarios about Roland. Should we catch him and burn him like we did Darby? Wouldn't that just release whatever is stuck inside?

"What do we do now?" Jamie asks, cutting into my thoughts. "Do we just wait until Ford questions us? What does he need from me? I barely knew Dixie. I only met her the one time Graham brought her to show her a project we were working on."

"That was this house," Graham says quietly. "I wanted to show her the kitchen we put in."

I chew my lip, thinking about that coincidence. "Who knew you brought her here?" I ask.

"No one, I guess. I mean, it wasn't a secret or anything," Graham says.

"The roofer was here that day," Jamie says. "I remember because he commented on how interesting Dixie looked after you two left. He thought she was cute."

"What is this roofer's name?" I ask, excited for a tiny lead that might take the heat off of Graham.

"Jason Flanagan. He couldn't have done this. He's worked for us for years," Jamie says. "He's a good guy."

"You never can tell. He knew of Dixie and knows this house. It's at least worth looking into."

"Man, I hate this," Graham says. "First, Dixie is dead, then we have to start looking at people we know and wondering if they're the killer. I really don't think Jason would hurt anyone."

"We have to tell Ford, either way," I say, glancing down the block to where Ford stands talking to Tyler. Ford looks so handsome it makes my heart hurt.

This breakup can't be the end. He's being unreasonable and he'll figure it out.

I have to have hope for that.

As I watch, the fire chief, Aiden Andrews, joins Ford. He feels me watching and smiles my way. I smile back, a reflex.

Ford looks over his shoulder at me, a slight scowl on his face.

Aiden says a few words to Ford, then walks my way.

"I thought you left," he says. "Things are pretty much wrapped up around here."

Most of the fire trucks have left and only the coroner's van and a few police cruisers remain. Even the crowd of onlookers has mostly dispersed. I check their faces, upset I didn't search them earlier. Arsonists love to watch their handiwork and are often in the crowd.

Is that what Roland was doing? Watching his work burn?

"I was waiting with my friends. This is Jamie and Graham. They own this house," I say.

"Oh, I'm so sorry for this. It must be a big blow to you."

"Not as much as losing Dixie," Graham says.

"Yeah," he says soberly. "You really talked to her ghost?" Aiden asks me.

"I did," I say with a touch of pride. "She was only here for a few minutes before she crossed."

"You saw her cross over?" he asks with awe.

"Yes. It's kind of what I do. I help the spirits cross to the other side. I have a YouTube show all about it, *Beyond the Dead*."

"I think I heard something about that. You're getting famous around here."

I give a little laugh. "Not really famous, but we do okay."

"We?"

"My best friend and partner, Mickey Ramirez. We do the show together."

"Can she see ghosts too?"

"No, she can't. I talk to the ghosts, and she tapes it for the show."

"How fascinating. I'll have to check it out." He raises a hand and waves to the coroner's van as it drives away.

"Looks like the scene is about wrapped up," I say.

"Pretty much." He checks his watch. "Sun's going to be up

soon. I could really use a coffee before I tackle the paperwork on this."

There's a question in his eyes that I don't quite understand.

"You should get one," I say, a bit uncertain.

"Want to join me?" His smile is bright and his brown eyes twinkle.

I'm so surprised, I don't answer at first. I glance down the sidewalk to Ford. He's watching us with angry eyes. I don't like his expression.

Aiden sees where I'm looking. "I'm sorry. I thought you said you weren't with him."

I push my hair over my shoulder. "I'm not. Not anymore."

"So coffee?"

"I know just the place." I'm surprised to feel a smile on my face.

The smile disappears when Ford walks over. "Time to go to the precinct," he says to Graham. "You too," he adds to Jamie. He doesn't even look at me or Aiden.

"Okay," Graham says, turning pale.

"They're just going to ask you questions. You did nothing wrong, so try not to worry," I say. Ford shoots me a look, his eyes then flicking to Aiden next to me.

I'm afraid he's going to put Graham in a squad car, but he just leads them to their car.

"I'm trusting you'll go directly there. I'll be right behind you the whole time."

"They aren't criminals," I tell him.

"Maybe not, but right now, he's a person of interest at the very least. You just go have your coffee and don't worry about it." He walks stiffly away.

I really don't like his dismissive attitude. I want to remind him he's the one that broke up with me. If I want to have coffee with someone, I can. But I don't get the chance to say anything. He climbs into his car and shuts the door without looking back.

Aiden and I watch the car drive away. Everyone else at the scene has left. We're alone as the sun begins to rise, pinking the sky.

"Look, I didn't mean to cause you trouble," Aiden says. "I just thought it might be nice to learn more about your work."

Ford's taillights turn at the corner. "No trouble," I say. "Have you been to The Hole?"

"Across from the courthouse, right?"

"Right. My aunt owns it."

"I love that place. I'll meet you there."

The town is just beginning to stir as I drive my old Cadillac through Ashby. I keep my eyes peeled for the puppet but don't see him anywhere. I really have no idea what to do about him being loose. I don't suppose he will just stay out of trouble and leave people alone. I have to stop him somehow.

A huge yawn catches me by surprise. I suddenly realize how very tired I am after basically being up all night. Maybe I should have turned Aiden down and just gone home to bed.

I mean, what am I doing?

I don't want any other man besides Ford. Even if he's mad at me right now.

Still, a bear claw and one of Aunt Val's super strong espressos should perk me up. If I get to talk to a nice person while I drink it, that's a good thing.

I pull into the last parking spot in front of The Hole. Aiden waits by the back of his truck for me to get out.

I resist the urge to check my reflection in the rearview mirror, but I do run my fingers through my hair to tame it.

The smile on his face makes me smile back.

"I could really use one of your aunt's Americanos right now," he says as he holds the door open for me.

"It's definitely been a long night," I say as we approach the counter. We are the only customers, and no one is behind the counter at the moment.

"Aunt Val?" I call.

"Coming," she replies and a moment later she appears from the back room. She does a double take when she sees me with Aiden.

"Good morning, Rylan," she says. "Chief Andrews," she adds with a nod. "What are you two doing up so early?" she asks. I know she has more questions, but she won't ask them in front of Aiden.

"We just came from a house fire where a woman was killed," I say quietly.

"How awful! I haven't heard about it yet. Of course, I just opened. I'm sure it will be all the talk today."

The door opens and the first customers enter, two tired-looking men in suits, no doubt men that work at the courthouse. They look like they're in a hurry.

Aiden and I step aside and let Aunt Val serve them first. Once the men leave, she asks, "Do you know who the victim was?"

"I talked to her ghost before she crossed. Her name is Dixie Campbell. Turns out she was the ex-girlfriend of my friend Graham. He and Jamie are the house flippers I told you about. They even own the house that burned. It was listed for sale."

"Oh, that can't be good for your friend." Val twists her hands in her green apron. "I sure hope they don't rush to judgment on him." There's an edge to her voice that I don't blame her for. She's forgiven Ford and Tyler for arresting her when she was innocent, but just barely.

"He's being questioned right now. I hope they go easy on him. Graham was so scared."

Val looks pointedly at Aiden, her eyebrows raised a fraction. I'm sure she's wondering why I'm here with a different man, but she's too polite to ask.

"Can I get a bear claw and an espresso, and Aiden, you wanted an Americano, right?"

Aiden has been standing patiently, silently letting us talk. He perks up now. "Yes, please. That sounds wonderful right now."

We settle into the corner booth by the window with our drinks and my pastry and Aiden says, "Tell me about your show. *Beyond the Dead*, right? That's a great name."

I warm at the praise, but before I can answer, the shop door opens and a man calls my name.

SEVEN

RYLAN FLYNN

I spin in my seat, startled by a man in a blue uniform. For a moment, I think it's a police officer and I panic, thinking something happened to Ford and they came to find me. Then I realize the uniform says "Security" and I recognize the man.

"Stan, hi," I say to the security guard that works at the courthouse.

Stan's head swivels from me to Aiden and back. "I was pretty sure that was your car out front, and I thought maybe I could catch you here. I hope that's okay?" he says tentatively.

"It's fine. What's up?"

Stan looks Aiden over carefully, no doubt taking in his uniform shirt with the Ashby Fire Department emblem on the chest.

"Can we talk outside?" Stan asks.

I give Aiden an apologetic look.

"Go ahead," he says. "I really should be getting back to the station anyway. Lots to do." He stands, then waits for me to stand too. Out on the sidewalk, he waves goodbye and says, "Good luck with the show," then heads off to his car.

"Sorry I intruded on your date," Stan says.

"It wasn't a date," I begin, then decide I don't need to explain myself. "You needed something?"

"Yes, I do. I mean—" he stammers.

"You came over here to talk to me. What was it?" I prompt the obviously uncomfortable man.

"I saw her," he says in a low whisper, looking around to make sure no one can hear.

"Saw who?" I'm too tired to play guessing games.

"The ghost at the courthouse. You know how I've told you I thought the courthouse was haunted? Well, I saw the ghost. At least, I think so."

I'm instantly awake. "I've seen her too. A woman in a torn red dress?"

"I didn't get that good of a look at her. Mostly just a shadowy shape, but I knew what it was when I saw it." He looks around again and waits for a couple entering The Hole to pass. "She's not dangerous, is she?"

"I don't think so. Most spirits just want peace." I think of Roland the marionette. Does he just want peace too? I've lived with his howls so long I'm sure what he wants is chaos and fear.

"Can you, you know, get rid of her? I've seen all your shows, that's what you do."

"It is what I do. I'll talk to my partner, Mickey, and see if we can get it scheduled. Could be tricky seeing as she's in the courthouse." I inwardly groan. My brother, Keaton, works for the district attorney at the courthouse. He would lose his mind if he found out I was filming a show there.

"We could do it after-hours. I have all the keys. You have to get rid of her. She's freaking me out."

I'm surprised the burly security guard is frightened of a shadowy shape. "She isn't hurting anyone."

"Not yet," he says with a little shake. "But a ghost at the courthouse? We can't have that. It's my job to keep it safe. A ghost roaming the halls can't be safe."

"Okay, okay, I'll see what I can do," I promise. Across the yard in front of the courthouse, I spot Keaton walking toward the entrance. I know the sun is up, but I'm surprised to see him at work so early.

Then I remember the murder, shocked I had forgotten about Dixie even for a short time. "Look, Stan, I need to go. It will be all over town soon, but there was a murder last night and an arson."

"Another murder? What is happening to this town? It's like it has turned evil or something."

My thoughts exactly.

And that evil is just going to get worse now that it's escaped Keaton's room.

More customers pour into The Hole as I watch Stan cross to the courthouse to go to work. I wish it was quieter. I'd love to talk to Aunt Val about Roland. Maybe she'd have some insight.

I look through the front window and see a line at the counter. Eileen, Val's assistant, is helping her. I debate getting behind the counter to help out too, like I have a few times, but they seem to have a handle on it. Just another busy morning for them.

Instead, I drive across town to Mickey's. I have a lot I need to talk out, and who better than my best friend to talk with? She's been with me through all the ghost hunting adventures. If anyone knows what to do about Roland, it will be Mickey.

I let myself through Mickey's front door, calling, "It's Rylan." Only then do I remember it's really early in the morning; Mickey may be sleeping. Her husband, Marco, is most definitely still asleep as he works late evenings at the school as a janitor.

The house is quiet and, disappointed, I turn to leave.

Then I hear a toilet flush and Mickey appears in the hall a few moments later.

"Hey," she says, surprised.

"Sorry, I should have called first. I just came over."

"You know you're always welcome." She pulls the bedroom door closed in the hall, then joins me in the front room. "What's up?" She sniffs. "You smell like a campfire."

I sniff my hair; it does indeed smell like smoke. "I was at a house fire," I say simply.

Mickey stares at me for a long moment. "We're going to need coffee, aren't we?"

"Strong coffee," I say. The espresso I drank at The Hole is singing in my blood, but the exhaustion is catching up to me.

I follow Mickey into the kitchen as she turns on the coffee maker. "I've hardly seen you," she says. "Thanks for texting me about catching Kenzie's killer last night. I appreciate it." She glances out of the corner of her eye. "I'm guessing you didn't go home and sleep afterward."

"Not exactly," I say sarcastically. This feels good being in Mickey's kitchen. Her house is clean and neat, the exact opposite of mine. It feels more like home than my own house.

"You look like you could fall over. Go sit on the couch and I'll bring this to you."

I want to argue, but the couch sounds wonderful. I pull off my leather jacket and I sink into the deep cushions. I lean my head back as my tired mind swirls. How am I going to explain everything to Mickey?

Start at the beginning and trust God to do the rest, Dad would tell me.

That's easy for him to say. He's a pastor, he and God are close. Besides, I don't think Dad has ever had to deal with a possessed puppet.

"Here's your coffee," Mickey says, and my eyes fly open. I hadn't realized I'd closed them. I push to sit up straight and take the hot mug.

Mickey settles into the recliner nearby, then says, "Okay, spill it. Why have you been up all night and why are you here so early? Did something happen with Ford? I thought you two were all lovey-dovey now."

"Well, yes, something happened with Ford, but that's not why I'm here," I start. I take a fortifying sip of my coffee. "What I'm going to tell you is sure to sound crazy, but you have to believe me."

"I always believe you." She's right. Ever since we were in school, Mickey has blindly believed me about all the nuts stuff I've told her. She's the best kind of friend.

I dive into the story of Roland. I skirt around Elsa's involvement and leave Mom completely out of it. As much as I trust Mickey, I'm not ready to talk about Mom's ghost. She'll ask why I haven't helped her cross and I don't want to look at my reasons too closely.

When I finish explaining, Mickey takes a long drink of her coffee. "This puppet, Roland, is out in Ashby right now doing who knows what?"

"Yes." I sit forward, excited she didn't doubt my sanity.

"That doesn't explain why you smell like smoke."

"That's a whole other story and also related, I think." I tell her about Dixie and Graham and seeing Roland at the fire.

Mickey just keeps sipping her coffee from her red mug, looking at me. Silence fills the living room when I finally stop talking.

"Wow, you have been busy," she says.

I lean back on the couch. "You could say that. I didn't even tell you about Ford breaking up with me and Aiden taking me for coffee. Then there's Stan and his ghost at the courthouse," I say sleepily.

"Rylan, only you." Another comfortable silence. "Wait, who's Aiden?"

"The fire chief. He asked me out for coffee this morning and I went. That's where I just came from."

"You went? What about Ford?"

"He wasn't happy. But, hey, he broke up with me. If he doesn't want me and Aiden wanted to be nice, who am I to say no?"

"We both know you and Ford will get back together. You two have been playing this game so long it's going to come around again."

"In my heart of hearts, I truly hope so," I say quietly, tipping my head back on the cushion. "It just hurts. I guess I wanted to hurt him back."

"That's understandable," Mickey says. Despite the espresso and the coffee, my limbs feel heavy. I sit my mug on the side table and snuggle deeper into the couch, my eyes blinking slowly.

"You're beat. Why don't you take a little nap and we can talk later?" Mickey says, handing me a throw pillow.

I take the pillow and curl up on the couch. "If you don't mind."

"Of course not." She covers me with a blue and white crocheted blanket. "Just rest."

I open my mouth to answer, but it seems like too much work. I let myself drift into a world where marionettes don't roam and bodies aren't burned.

EIGHT

RYLAN FLYNN

I wake to hushed voices coming from the kitchen. I can't catch most of the words, but I hear Marco saying something about a puppet.

I'd rather curl back into the couch and drift off again, but I sit up and rub my eyes instead. I check the time. It's almost noon. I can't believe I slept so long, but the rest did me good.

"You don't really believe this crazy story, do you?" Marco asks Mickey.

"She's never lied to me before," Mickey defends me.

I feel bad that I can overhear them, so I clear my throat loudly. They both stop talking immediately. Mickey looks out from the kitchen. "You're up."

"Yeah. Thanks for letting me sleep. I really needed that." I fold the blue and white blanket and drape it across the back of the couch.

"You're always welcome here. You know that. I was just making some lunch. You hungry?"

"Famished," I say, following her back into the kitchen where she returns to making sandwiches. "Hey, Marco," I say. He leans against the sink, a glass of tea in his hand.

"Did you have a good nap?" he asks as friendly as ever, like he didn't just basically call me a crazy liar a minute ago.

"Sorry to crash on you guys. I'm guessing Mickey told you what's going on."

Marco takes a drink, studying me over the rim of the glass. "A possessed puppet?" he asks with the barest touch of sarcasm. "I know you two see a lot of stuff, but really?" The sarcasm grows heavier.

"I know it's hard to believe, but we had a possessed bear a short while ago. This one isn't nice, though, and it's loose in town right now. I don't know what to do to catch it."

He takes another drink as he weighs his words. "If, and I mean, *if*, this puppet is real, you have to figure out what it wants."

"It's only ever wanted to terrorize me. It's been locked in Keaton's room for years. It likes to laugh and howl."

"For years?" Mickey asks, the knife she was spreading mayonnaise with frozen above the bread. "And you never told me?"

"I didn't tell anyone. What was I supposed to say?"

"True, I guess. But I would have helped you," she says, the hurt obvious.

"I'm sorry. You're right. I didn't know what to do with it. At least it was contained."

"How did it get out?" Marco asks. "Why now?"

I tell them about Elsa moving the boxes and how she's staying at the house, but leave out the part about Mom. They've had enough revelations for today.

"I'm glad Elsa is safe," Mickey says. "I didn't like the thought of her floating around with nowhere to go."

"She's safe," I say.

"Unless this puppet wants her," Marco says.

"Why would it want her?" I ask, genuinely curious.

"An innocent soul? Sounds like just the thing an evil spirit would want. That's how it would be in a movie."

"Babe, be serious. This isn't a movie," Mickey says.

Now that he's said it, the worry charges in. "He ran out of the house and was at the fire last night. If he wanted Elsa, he could have taken her instead of escaping."

"Maybe he hasn't figured it out yet." Marco finishes his drink and sets the empty glass in the sink. "I'm just throwing ideas out. This is my first evil spirit possession."

"I appreciate the help," I say. "This is my first evil spirit too, well, I guess, not exactly."

"What do you mean?" Mickey asks as she hands me a sandwich.

"Every time we've faced a murderer recently, there's been an object with some sort of evil inside it. I've destroyed them as I can, but I think it's related to the thing that's in Roland."

"Have you told Ford about all this?" Marco asks.

"He knows most of it."

"Well, there you go. Let him handle it. Catching bad guys is his job."

"I don't think this is a matter for the police. How would he explain it even if he wanted?"

"Rylan is really the best one to handle this," Mickey says.

"Maybe, but you don't have to be involved. This isn't something you should put on your show. Ghosts are one thing, people understand that they may exist. But you can't put a marionette on the show. You'll be laughed at and destroy all you've built."

"Yeah, that wouldn't go well. Viewers would think we faked it," Mickey agrees.

"I can't really think about the show right now. Stan at the courthouse has a ghost he wants us to check out that would make a good episode. But with Roland and also Dixie's murder,

Stan will have to wait." I take the last bite of my sandwich. "I really should be going."

"What are you going to do?" Mickey asks, following me into the living room.

"Honestly, I don't know," I say, picking up my jacket and sliding it on.

"If you need anything, don't hesitate to ask." Mickey looks toward the kitchen. "He's just being protective," she says in a low voice.

"I don't blame him. Really, I don't. I just have to find Roland before he can do any more damage. I have a strong suspicion that he's either influencing the arsonist that killed Dixie or he did it himself. I have to stop him." I open the front door.

"Keep me posted," Mickey says. "Good luck."

"Yeah, good luck," Marco calls from the doorway of the kitchen. The look on his face says, *Don't come back.*

I let Mickey close the door behind me and look around the neighborhood. Where could Roland be? Where do I start?

Start at the beginning and trust God to do the rest, Dad's words echo in my head again.

I suddenly want Dad. He's the only person I can think of that has experience with spirits. He's often by my side when we cross lost souls. This is a little different, but I know he'd understand.

His church is only a few blocks away and I make the drive easily. I'm pleased to see his car in the parking lot. He's the only one here. Just the way I'd hoped.

I keep my head down as I walk through the small cemetery in front of the church, not wanting to see any ghosts that might be lingering. Luckily, I make it to the wide wooden doors without incident.

I let myself into the small building and close the door behind me. The silence of the church envelops me. The scent of the old building comforts me. The sound of my dad's voice down the hall on the right calls to me.

I knock on his office door and duck my head in. He's on the phone, but smiles when he sees me. "Look, I'll have to call you back," he says into the phone. "My daughter just stopped by."

He hangs up and motions for me to come in and take a seat. I pass the offered chair and go around his desk. Reading my intent, he stands to take me in his arms.

I sink into the familiar embrace, the scent of his cologne filling my nose just the way it has since I was a child. The scent is one I bought him for his birthday when I was in middle school. He's worn it ever since. I breathe deeply of the nostalgia.

"It's okay," he murmurs although I haven't said a word. "It will all be okay."

Tears suddenly come, surprising us both. I cling to my father, needing his strength. He pats my back like he did when I was a child.

The fatherly magic works.

I sniffle and lift my head from his chest. "Sorry," I mumble.

"Don't be sorry," he says, releasing me. "I haven't had a hug like that from you in a long time."

"I just—" I don't know where to start.

"Sit and tell me," he says, leading me to the small couch in the corner where he counsels parishioners.

I perch on the stiff green cushions and pull my jacket tight around me. Once I open my mouth, everything comes out. Ford breaking up with me, Elsa releasing Roland, Dixie and the fire. All the mess of the last several hours.

When I finally stop talking, he takes a moment to let it sink in.

"That's all?" he asks, trying for a joke.

It's lame, but it makes me smile. "Yeah, just a few things."

"Well," he sits back, "let's start at the beginning. You can't fix Ford. That boy loves you and will come to his senses when the time is right."

"I knew you'd say something like that."

"Elsa didn't know what she was doing when she released the puppet, and what's done is done now. You will have to cross that poor girl soon. She can't stay on this side."

"You're right. I just wanted to reunite her with her parents first."

"That might not be possible, but we'll deal with that soon enough. The real threat is Roland and how he might be influencing the arsonist that killed Dixie or worse."

"Right." I run my hands down my thighs. "I don't know what to do to stop him. Marco says I need Ford to do it since he is the police. But that won't work. It's my fault Roland is here, so I need to stop him."

"How is it your fault? You didn't create him. Only God can create."

"Even evil?"

"Evil is just a balance of good. We can't have one without the other."

This strikes a chord. "So if my powers are for good, his powers are for bad?"

"That's one way to look at it. Keaton did bring that puppet home not too long after your accident where you got your powers. They could be related."

"I don't like this," I say. "I don't want to be tied to that thing in any way."

"Honey, you don't have a choice. Your gift is your destiny. Just like facing the thing inside the puppet is your destiny."

I shake my head. "Holy flip, this sucks."

"Yeah. Our callings can be difficult. You already know that. But you've risen to every challenge God has given you so far. This will be no different."

"What if I'm not up for it?"

"You will be when the time is right."

"You sound like a fortune cookie," I tease.

"A little, but that doesn't make me wrong," he says, patting me on the knee.

"So, what do I do?"

"Maybe you need to talk to Keaton. The puppet is his after all."

"You just want to force us to be together."

"Is that so bad to want my kids to get along? I don't understand why you two are always at each other's throats all the time."

"You'd have to ask him."

"I have. He says I have to ask you."

I'm not liking the turn this conversation has taken, but he's right. Keaton should know more about the puppet than I do. I've barely seen it, have only kept it locked away. He slept with it in his room growing up.

The thought makes me shiver. Did Keaton know what it truly was?

I stand with a purpose. I'm certainly going to find out.

NINE
FORD PIERCE

The man across the interrogation table from me doesn't look like a killer. He looks scared. My instincts tell me he didn't hurt Dixie, but my instincts could be wrong. Too often a significant other is the perpetrator of a violent crime. An ex significant other is even higher on the list.

Tyler and I have questioned him from every angle we can think of, but Graham sticks to his story. He hasn't seen Dixie in months and has no idea what happened to her or why she was found in a house he owns.

"I'm telling you, I did not hurt Dixie," he says for at least the dozenth time. "Please, you have to believe me."

We're getting nowhere, and when Tyler gives me a look, I know he feels it too.

"Okay, if we choose to believe you," Tyler says, "who do you think might have hurt her? This lead on the roofer is a weak one, so is the coworker. We'll look into them, of course, but does anyone else come to mind?"

Graham sits back in his chair and crosses his arms. "I'm done talking. I don't know anything about Dixie's life now or what happened to her. All this is just coincidence."

We don't have enough to hold him, so we have to let him go. He hurries from the room like a scared rabbit.

"Well, that was a bust," I say, tired and cranky. "I don't think he's our guy."

"Me either," Tyler agrees. "We should still keep an eye on him, just in case, but I doubt it leads to anything."

"There has to be a reason she was burned in his house. I don't believe in coincidences like that."

Tyler rubs the back of his neck. "Maybe we're looking at this wrong. He's not the only owner of the house. Maybe Jamie is the key."

I have an even harder time seeing the petite redhead as a killer.

"Hear me out," Tyler says, warming to the idea. "She's jealous of Dixie's relationship with Graham, so she eliminates her. She then burns her own house down for insurance money."

"That's a little far-fetched. Dixie and Graham weren't even together anymore. Why hurt her?"

"It's weak, but it's as possible as the coworker. We have to look at every angle."

"We've already talked to Jamie. She's as confused by all this as Graham is."

"Yeah." Tyler seems defeated. "We can keep that idea on the table, but it's unlikely."

"We need more information. While we wait on the warrant for her phone records, let's go check out Dixie's apartment."

Tyler quickly stands, as anxious as I am to get out of this tiny interrogation room.

Dixie's apartment is in a small complex of only twenty or so units, all with ground-floor entrances and walkways to the front doors. Her unit is already taped off and a few officers are milling about as well as crime scene techs working the scene. Officer James Frazier approaches.

"Detectives," he says. "We got the scene locked down and the techs are here. Honestly, there isn't much to see. No forced entry and little in the way of a struggle visible. The coffee table is pushed crooked, but it's hard to tell if that happened last night or if it's just how she kept it."

We follow Frazier into the apartment. Besides a pile of laundry on the couch, the small unit is neat and tidy. The coffee table is shoved sideways by a few inches, but everything else seems to be in its place. The bed is made and the bathroom is unremarkable.

I spend several moments just taking in the scene trying to visualize what might have happened. Two techs work the scene, but I doubt they'll find anything.

One, Michelle, talks to Tyler in the kitchen. Her smile is too bright for a crime scene, but I can't blame her. It's obvious the two like each other. I think they even went for coffee once.

Coffee.

I think of Rylan out with Aiden. How could she?

"What have you found?" I demand of Michelle when I walk into the tiny kitchen.

Her smile instantly falters. "Um, right. We honestly haven't found much. We took some fingerprints, but we'll have to check them against the victim's to know if they mean anything."

"That's great," Tyler says, trying to lighten the mood. "We appreciate all your hard work."

"Yes, thank you." I try to smooth the situation. Michelle didn't deserve me talking to her like that.

"I wish we had more," she says.

"You can't find evidence that isn't here. We don't really even know that she was attacked here. Just because Rylan said it doesn't mean it's true," I say.

"Rylan said?" Michelle asks. "Did she talk to the victim's ghost?"

"Yeah," Tyler says. "She saw her before she crossed. Dixie said she remembers being here, then being in the house on fire."

"Wild," Michelle says with obvious approval. "Did she say who hurt her?"

"No," I say shortly. "Guess we'll have to do the police work and not rely on Rylan for a change." I regret the harshness of my tone the moment the words leave my mouth. Everything with Rylan is irritating me this morning. First, her stunt last night that nearly got her killed, then her inserting herself into yet another case. Then she goes for coffee with Aiden Andrews of all people.

Aiden was two years ahead of me in high school. He was the typical all-American hero. Basketball star and good-looking. If I'm honest, I was a little envious of him back then.

Now he's asked Rylan out. Seriously?

"We always do the police work," Tyler says, defensive.

"I know." I rub my hand over the stubble growing on my cheek. I'm tired and irritable and taking it out on my team. This is unacceptable. "I'm going to look around outside."

The late morning air is growing warm, the sun shining bright. I take a moment to just breathe, my eyes closed. Dixie is relying on me to focus.

"Detective Pierce?" A woman's voice. I open my eyes with a start. "I'm sorry, I didn't mean to startle you." Faith Hudson stands on the walkway. She was moved up to detective on our last case, but I'm surprised to see her here.

"Hudson," I say. "Good to see you."

"I hope this isn't going to be awkward, but Chief sent me over. He wants all three of us on this case."

"All three of us?"

"He says with the arson on top of the homicide, he needs us all."

And a possessed puppet running around if Rylan can be believed, but I'm not going to tell her that. I haven't even told Tyler, and he's used to all the paranormal stuff where Rylan is concerned.

I shake Faith's hand and force myself to be nice. "Welcome to the team. There's not much to see inside. Scene is clean. Let's go talk to the neighbors."

Before Faith and I can begin canvassing the neighborhood, a young woman with a purple streak in her hair waves to catch our attention from the other side of the yellow tape.

"Are you detectives?" she asks, her eyes huge with worry. "This is Dixie's apartment. What's with the yellow tape and detectives? Dixie's okay, right?"

"Do you know Dixie?" I ask.

"We're friends and we work together at the salon. She didn't come to work today and wasn't answering her phone, so I left the shop and came to check on her. Please tell me she's all right."

"I'm so sorry, but Dixie has passed away," Faith says gently.

"Passed? What?" The woman nearly collapses, but Faith steadies her. "What happened? Why all the police?"

"It's really too early to say," Faith hedges. "What's your name? Let's start with that."

"Rebecca," she sniffles.

I perk up at this. The coworker that Graham said Dixie had the run-in with. "How long have you known Dixie?" I ask.

"Just a few months since I started at the salon."

"Were you close?" Faith asks.

"Yes. I mean, for coworkers. We hung out a few times after work. I'd like to say we were friends."

"We heard you had a run-in with Dixie. Over a man, I believe."

Rebecca looks startled. "That was nothing really. Just a misunderstanding. We became pretty good friends after that.

Besides, she and Graham broke up not long after." Rebecca wipes at her eyes. "Can you tell me anything? Was she murdered?" She whispers the last word.

This piques my attention. "Why would you say that?"

Rebecca is surprised by my question. "Why else would you all be here? Detectives don't come to apartments if she died in a car accident or something."

"Rebecca, can you think of anyone that might want to hurt Dixie?" Faith asks.

"No. No one comes to mind."

"No strange customers that might be too friendly with her? No exes she had issues with?"

"Dixie didn't have issues like that. Not that I know of. As for customers, we all have a few that get a bit too attached. I wouldn't say any of them stand out as dangerous."

"And exes?" Faith asks.

"I don't know of any issues there either. As far as I know, Graham was the last man you'd call a boyfriend. That ended a while ago."

"Was she dating anyone new recently?" I ask.

Rebecca chews on her thumbnail nervously, thinking. "There's this one guy that she's gone out with a few times. I don't know his name. She was kind of hush-hush about it. I saw her talking to him in the parking lot once."

"How do you know they were dating?" Faith asks.

"Not sure they were dating, but she was happier the last weeks or so, you know how it is with a new man." Rebecca looks to Faith for confirmation.

"Is that all? She was happier and you saw her with a man in a parking lot?" I push.

"Well, it's the way she was with him. Leaning in while they were talking, touching his chest. I could tell she liked him."

"What did he look like?" I ask.

"Dark hair, short, but longer than yours. He had a beard.

Not one of those bushy ones. It was trimmed neat. And he wore wire-rim glasses."

"You just described Graham Rock," I say.

"It wasn't Graham, but now that you mention it, they looked very similar. I guess Dixie had a type."

"Have you seen this man any other time?" Faith asks.

"I just saw him the one time. Like I said, she didn't really talk about him. I don't even think she knows I saw her with him," Rebecca says.

"Where were you last night?" I ask, changing tactics.

Rebecca seems surprised, runs her hand over the purple streak in her hair. "I was on a date."

"Will he verify you were with him?" I ask.

"I hope so. It was our first date, and I doubt he'll be happy about being questioned by the police. I wasn't planning on seeing him again anyway."

"Why's that?" Faith asks.

"I found out he has a girlfriend about halfway through the date. He actually told me. I swear it's not easy to find a good guy these days."

"What's his name?" I ask.

"Travis Cobb. Here's his number."

"What time did you end the date with Travis?" Faith asks.

"Just after he told me about his girlfriend. Jerk seemed proud of it. Like he was getting one over on her or something. I made up an excuse and got out of there."

"Where did you go?" I ask.

"The Lock Up. I should have known the date would go badly when he took me to a bar."

"What time did you leave?" I ask.

"About ten, I guess."

"Dixie wasn't found until nearly 4 a.m.," I say.

"Okay?" Rebecca says.

"Can you account for your whereabouts between ten and four?" I push.

She pales. "No. I went home. I told you, I would never have hurt Dixie. She was my friend."

I believe the petite woman. She may have been able to hurt Dixie, but whoever did it moved the body to that house and set it on fire. I don't think Rebecca would have the strength to move her. "We'll have more questions for you. We'll be in touch soon," I say, handing her my card. "Call if you think of anything helpful. Anything at all."

Rebecca takes the card with the tips of her fingers. She chews on her lower lip in thought. "I'm sure this is nothing, but since you said anything."

"Go ahead," Faith says.

"I saw Dixie with Graham about a week ago. At least I think I did. It was at the gas station. They were talking at the pumps. I'm sure they just bumped into each other, but I thought I'd mention it."

"Do you think Graham had something to do with this?" I ask.

"I wouldn't know, but it's usually a current boyfriend or an ex, isn't it?"

TEN

RYLAN FLYNN

I keep wanting to turn the car and head for home instead of talking to Keaton, but I know Dad is right.

Keaton brought the puppet home. He lived with it in his room for a few years before he went off to college. Even then, he spent holidays and summers with the thing still in his room.

He has to know there's something wrong with it.

For the second time today, I park in the town square. Although I can smell Aunt Val's donuts, now is not the time for a snack.

I run a hand through my hair and it snags. I can barely remember the last time I brushed my hair, let alone took a shower. I feel like a mess, and I know I still smell like smoke.

I gather the tangle of my hair back into a low ponytail and call it good.

The afternoon sun is warmer than usual, and I wish I had left my jacket in the car as I make my way down the sidewalk to the front door of the courthouse.

Stan is working the security checkpoint and brightens when he sees me. "You came," he says, after I walk through the scanner. He looks around to be sure we're not overheard, then says in a low voice, "I haven't seen her today."

I'd forgotten that I'd have to see Stan in order to talk to Keaton. "I'm actually here to see my brother, but I will be back about your—" Someone enters the front door. "Your concern."

"He came in early. He's up on the second floor."

"Thanks." My voice sounds too loud in the hushed courthouse. Trying not to give into my nerves, I make my way up the wide, limestone stairs. I keep an eye out for the lady in the red dress, but I don't see her.

Good. I'm not ready to deal with her just yet. She's been here for a hundred years based on the 1920s style of her dress. She can wait a while longer.

I find the DA's office and hesitate outside the double doors. I've never visited Keaton at work before and I'm showing up unannounced. With a murder investigation going on today, I doubt he'll be happy for a little family reunion.

I think of the puppet and how horrible he is and how the town might be in danger, and I pull the door open.

The receptionist sits just inside. Cheryl Nelson, Keaton's fiancée. I'd like to say she and I are friends since she lives with and is engaged to my brother, but we aren't. I didn't even know she worked here.

"Hey, Cheryl," I say with as wide a smile as I can muster. Cheryl looks up from her computer, surprise dancing across her pretty face.

"Rylan? I sure didn't expect to see you here."

I'm suddenly self-conscious. Cheryl looks smart and put-together in her cream-colored blouse and tasteful jewelry. Part of my ponytail has escaped the tie and is floating across my forehead. "I didn't know you worked here," I blurt out.

"Yeah," she says with obvious pride. "Just a few weeks ago. The other receptionist quit, and Keaton told me to apply. I like it."

"I bet it's nice to see Keaton all day." I don't actually think that would be good, but she sees something in him I don't.

"I don't get to see him much. He's very busy. Especially today," she adds pointedly.

"I know he's busy, but I need to see him."

"Can't it wait until after work? I don't want to be rude, but family issues don't come before work here." She's trying to be nice about turning me away, but it rankles just the same.

"I can wait."

She gives me a tight smile. "I don't think that will help. Like I said, they're all really busy."

I'm beginning to see why Cheryl got this position. If part of the job description is turning undesirable people away, then she's great at it.

I want to rush past her desk and search for my brother, but I know that's a bad idea. Maybe coming here at all was a bad idea. If Keaton does know anything about the puppet's evil tendencies, he's not going to want to talk about it at work where people could overhear.

"Okay. I get it," I finally say. "Do you two have plans for later after work?"

Cheryl blinks in surprise. "Like dinner plans? No, I don't think so."

"Great. How about we meet at Aunt Val's cabin? I can ask him what I need there, and we can all discuss it."

"Now you have me intrigued," she says. "Discuss what?"

"Now's not the time for family issues," I say, throwing her own words back at her. "Just be at Aunt Val's at six thirty." I don't let her answer, I just exit the office. Far down the hall, staring at me, I see the woman in the torn red dress. She stares for a moment, then walks around a corner.

I should chase after her. Should find out what her story is.

I let her go. I have enough on my plate at the moment.

With a wave to Stan, I'm back outside. Aunt Val's is directly across the street. I hurry across and let myself into the donut shop. Val is behind the counter, looking a little more tired than she did first thing this morning.

"Hey, Rylan," she brightens. "Twice in one day?"

"Want to make it three times?" I ask.

"What do you mean?"

"I just invited Keaton and Cheryl over to your house tonight for dinner. I hope that's okay. There's something I need to talk to you all about, and I thought it would be easier to do at once."

"Sawyer was coming over tonight. But if you don't mind him being there, then sure, come on over."

It might be a good idea if Val's boyfriend is a part of this. He's open to ghosts and spirits and he's a smart man. Maybe he can help. "Sure, that would be great."

"Is everything okay?" she asks.

"Honestly, I don't know. Don't worry too much and I'll tell you all about it tonight."

ELEVEN

RYLAN FLYNN

My phone chirps as I climb into my car. It's Jamie.

Can we talk?

Of course, I text back.
Can you come over? She adds an address.
I had hoped to go home and check on Mom and Elsa, but if Jamie needs to talk right now, it can only be about Dixie.

Be right there.

It only takes a few minutes to find the address Jamie gave. I see her car parked in the short driveway and Graham's little SUV behind it. This is an older part of the town, and the house is similar to the ones they like to flip. A standard two-story with a small porch. Just like thousands of houses in small towns across America. Still, it has a warm, inviting air to it. Flowers in baskets on the porch and a flag that says "Welcome Home" hanging on the wall by the door.

I climb the two steps to the freshly painted porch and knock on the wooden door.

Jamie answers right away.

"Thanks for coming," she says, showing me into the living room where Graham is sitting on the couch with a yellow throw pillow on his lap. He grips the pillow nervously.

"What's going on?" I ask. Something touches my ankle and I jump. A fat orange cat pushes against me.

"That's Oscar," Jamie says. "Sorry, he doesn't know a stranger."

Seeing Oscar reminds me of Onyx, the cat that recently moved in with me. When's the last time I saw him? Does he need fed? I feel bad I'm not taking better care of him.

I bend to pat the cat on the head. "Have a seat," Jamie says as she settles in next to Graham.

I take the only other seat in the room, a small recliner. I perch on the edge as Oscar continues rubbing against my legs.

"Okay?" I ask. "What's up?"

Jamie looks at Graham. "He needs to tell us something. He wouldn't say anything until you got here."

Graham clears his throat. "I have an idea of what might have happened to Dixie," he says.

"Who?"

"Not a who, but a what." He sounds reluctant to talk. "This is going to sound nuts, but maybe not to you."

I lean forward. "You have my attention."

"I think a ghost may be trying to exact revenge. I know it sounds crazy, but it's the only thing that makes sense. You see, Eddie Weinman and I were best friends back in high school. He was like a brother to me."

"What happened?" Jamie asks.

"The whole family hates me now. They think I killed his sister, Maria."

Stunned silence fills the room.

"What do you mean?" Jamie asks. "What happened to Maria?"

My stomach sinks before he even answers. I know the name Maria Weinman.

Graham takes off his glasses and rubs his eyes in a gesture that's growing familiar. "You have to understand, I was only seventeen at the time. Maria was only fourteen, but she seemed much older. I saw her around a lot while hanging out with Eddie. I guess things sort of progressed from there."

"You were dating?" Jamie asks.

I keep silent. I know how this story ends, just didn't know Graham was part of it.

"Not dating, exactly, but we spent time together alone. I never touched her, not like that. We only kissed a few times. God, we were just kids." He falls quiet.

"You were at the quarry with her?" I ask after a long, heavy pause.

"We snuck up there to go swimming. No one was with us. No one knew we went. You know how there are these cliffs that the kids jump off of," he says to me.

"I know, but I've never been."

"I don't know. I didn't grow up around here," Jamie says, growing angry. "Is someone going to tell me what happened?"

"Maria and I held hands and jumped. She told me she wasn't a good swimmer, but I convinced her to jump anyway. Told her I'd keep her safe. I was so full of myself back then. Thought I was invincible."

"Did she drown?" Jamie asks.

"She went under when we landed, and I lost hold of her hand. I surfaced, but she didn't," his voice chokes.

"Jesus," Jamie says.

"I remember it. Maria was in the class ahead of me. I knew she was with a boy, but not that it was you," I say.

"That was me. They searched for her, but her body was never found. She just disappeared in the dark water."

"Oh, wow," Jamie says. "How awful for you."

"Eddie blamed me. His whole family did. That's why I say the Weinmans hate me. They think I killed her. No matter how many times I explained, they never believed it was an accident."

Jamie rubs him on the shoulder. "Of course it was an accident. There's no way you'd hurt her on purpose."

"Thank you," he says miserably. "Doesn't mean I didn't blame myself. Maria would never have been there if it wasn't for me."

"You think Eddie might be the one trying to frame you?"

"No. It can't be. Eddie never recovered from losing Maria. He took his own life a few years later. I suppose his ghost could have come back to hurt me, but I don't think he would do that."

"Oh man," Jamie says.

"And last I heard, her parents moved away. She had an older brother that was away at college at the time."

"Maybe it's him?" I ask.

"Last I heard, Dillon was in jail. So it can't be him."

The room grows quiet, the sunlight too bright for the story he's telling. I mull over what he said.

"You think Maria's ghost has come to get revenge?" I ask, putting the pieces together.

"It crossed my mind. I've seen your show, and sometimes ghosts can move things. Maybe she's super strong and she murdered Dixie and burned the house down." He sounds desperate.

I hate to dash his hopes. "I suppose anything is possible. But I really don't think a ghost would murder an innocent woman just to get back at you. Especially the ghost of a fourteen-year-old girl," I say gently.

"It must not be related to that tragedy," Jamie says. "It has to be someone else." Oscar jumps on her lap. "Wait, what about Travis?"

Graham perks up. "Why didn't I think of that? He's the type to hurt a woman and he's definitely not happy with me right now."

"Who's Travis?"

"Travis Cobb. He's dating my sister, Evie. I wish she'd break up with him, but she thinks she's in love. I found out he's been cheating on her, and we had a little conversation about it. At one point, he took a swing at me. I had to fight back. I bloodied his nose. He called me all kinds of names and said Evie could make her own decisions. That was really the end of it."

"When was this?" I ask.

"A week ago."

"It's a long shot, but we should tell Ford anyway. It could be Travis doing this to you."

"Do you really think someone is framing Graham?" Jamie asks after a long moment. "I mean, couldn't it be someone mad with Dixie and burning our house is just a coincidence?"

"Do you believe that?" I ask.

She looks down at Oscar. "Not really. It does feel too close to home. Maybe they're trying to frame me. The house is both of ours."

"You didn't know Dixie," I point out.

"I knew her a little. I mean, I do sort of look guilty." She starts to sound panicked.

"Now don't find problems where there aren't any. No one thinks you did this."

"I bet Ford and Tyler do." She pushes Oscar off her lap and stands. "What if they're coming for me now?"

"They already talked to you, didn't they? If they thought you were a viable suspect, you'd already know. You can't jump to conclusions like that. Both of you need to try and stay calm. Neither of you are guilty, so there isn't any evidence against you. We just need to figure out who *is* guilty so you can stop worrying."

They exchange looks, then Jamie sits back down, closer to Graham this time. I wonder how long it will take them to realize they like each other more than the business partners they are.

This of course leads my mind to Ford.

Always to Ford.

"I better get going," I say, standing. "I'll show myself out."

"Thank you for coming," Graham says. "I really thought I was onto something with the ghost theory."

"I mean, we can't rule it out. I think that whoever killed Dixie is flesh and blood and he will be brought to justice."

I let myself out the front door onto the lovely porch. The door closes behind me and I step to the walkway.

I need to call Ford.

I want to call Ford.

He'll only tell me to stay out of it.

That's a chance I'll have to take, but I chicken out at a live call. Instead, I send a text.

Graham had a fight with a Travis Cobb. You should look into him.

There, I told him.

Almost instantly I get a return text. *???*

I don't answer that. He'd only remind me he's the detective and I should stay home and just watch TV or knit or something.

Right now, I have a murder to help solve to clear my friends and a deranged puppet on the loose. Knitting will have to wait.

TWELVE

RYLAN FLYNN

I haven't been to Aunt Val's cabin in the woods for a while. As I drive through the trees, I feel myself relax, feel my heart slow down. This was a good idea. Even if nothing comes of talking to Keaton about Roland, at least I'll have an evening in a place of peace.

Mine is not the only car in the clearing and I surmise that Sawyer has already arrived. I'm glad for Aunt Val to have a new boyfriend and I like Sawyer, even if I haven't spent much time with him and none of it has been under normal circumstances.

Tonight won't be any different.

I hope what I'm about to tell them all doesn't scare him away from Val.

Val's big black lab mix, George, bounds off the porch to greet me. I give him a good rub, then climb the steps to the porch. I hear gravel crunching behind me. Keaton's silver BMW pulls in and parks right behind my beat-up Cadillac. There's plenty of room in the clearing, why did he have to park me in?

I push down my annoyance with my brother and try to focus on the mission ahead. I hurry across the porch and in the front door before he gets out of the car, hoping for a moment with Val.

The cabin smells wonderful, and I breathe deeply of the scent of frying bacon. Val is in the kitchen taking bacon out of an electric skillet as Sawyer slices tomatoes next to her, laughing softly together. I feel like I'm intruding.

"Hey," Val says with warmth. "Perfect timing. The BLTs are just about ready."

I take a seat at the kitchen bar sneaking a piece of bacon off the plate. It's the perfect amount of crispy and tastes delicious.

"I can't thank you enough for letting us meet here. I thought it might be easiest to do this all at the same time," I say.

"You have my curiosity on high, but I can wait until you're ready to share what this is about," Val says.

"Does it have to do with the fire and the murder this morning?" Sawyer asks.

"Sort of," I say. "I promise I'll explain everything, but can we eat first?"

"As soon as your brother gets here," Val says.

"He's coming now." As if on cue, the front door opens. "And there they are."

Keaton looks irritated as he enters, but his face brightens when he sees our aunt.

"BLTs?" he asks with obvious excitement as he and Cheryl fill the small cabin.

"Your favorite," Val says. I'd forgotten the sandwich is Keaton's favorite. If asked, I couldn't say what was his favorite anything. We've really grown apart. Not that we were ever close to begin with.

"Thanks for having us," Cheryl says to Val, taking off her jacket and hanging it on a dining room chair. Her sharp eyes land on me. I'm glad I took the time to stop by home to shower and change and feed Onyx. I look much better than the last time I saw her. "We don't have a lot of time. Keaton is very busy with this murder case, as I'm sure you know."

"I won't take too much time," I say, trying to keep the edge out of my voice.

"Let's eat first," Val says. "Everyone is busy, but food must be eaten. Come make your sandwich."

Once we're all settled at the table, an almost companionable silence falls over the cabin. I don't remember the last time I shared a meal with my brother and Cheryl. We used to have family breakfast here pretty regularly, but Keaton cancelled more and more often and he rarely brought Cheryl.

Sawyer, of course, is a new addition. He tries for small talk. "So, Rylan, how's the show going?"

I chew the bite of BLT in my mouth and swallow before answering. "It's going well. Our last episode really took off and we're getting bigger. I'm pretty excited about it."

"Over a million views," Val says with pride. "That is amazing."

"Yeah, good job," Keaton says without a trace of sarcasm, then pops the last of his sandwich into his mouth. After he swallows, he says, "Okay. Now what is this all about?"

I can't put this off any longer, so I dive in. "This is all going to sound crazy and like I'm making it up, but I promise you, it's real."

"Okay," Val says. "We all know you wouldn't make up a story."

I look to Keaton who is leaning back in his chair, arms crossed. "Do you remember a marionette you had when we were young?" I ask him.

A moment of fear flickers across his face so quickly I'm not sure I saw it. "I had a marionette, yes."

"Roland?" I say. "A jester with a painted face."

"Yes," he says with forced patience. "Why?"

"Did you ever feel something was strange about the puppet?

Did it do anything weird when you were still living in your old room?"

"What is this?" Cheryl asks. "You make us all come out here to talk about an old toy?"

"Let her finish," Val says.

Keaton looks uncomfortable. "I don't know what you mean." I think he does.

I take a deep breath and say, "The puppet is possessed. It has been for a long time. I want to know if you knew about it."

He shifts in his seat. "Possessed? That's preposterous."

"Is it?" I push.

Keaton looks from face to face. "Okay, so the puppet was creepy. I should have left it in the dump where I found it. I don't know about possessed, but I did have bad dreams about it back then. I was just a teenager. You know, impressionable and all that."

"Did it ever move?" I press.

"Seriously, Rylan. What are you talking about?" Cheryl asks.

"The puppet has been moving around for a long time. It even tried to escape the room. I kept it locked in there all this time. I put crosses all around the room, even on the window and door. It just kept getting stronger, louder. Now it has gotten loose."

A stunned silence fills the room.

"Loose as in out of the room?" Sawyer asks.

"Out of the house," I say. "It gets worse. The thing is evil. I know it. Whatever is inside the puppet is influencing the murderers that have been terrorizing the town recently. Every one that I've stopped had a cursed object that I destroyed."

Another long silence, broken when Keaton asks, "If you knew the puppet was evil, why didn't you destroy it too?"

A good question. Why didn't I?

"I was afraid of it. By the time I knew what it was, it had

grown too strong. Besides, if the evil was locked in your room, then it wasn't going to hurt anyone."

"How did it get out?" Val asks.

I'd hoped no one would ask this. "I have the ghost of a little girl at my house, Elsa. Roland tricked her into opening the door."

"You have a ghost living with you?" Keaton asks with derision. "Shouldn't you cross her over? That is what you do."

If he only knew Elsa wasn't alone. He'd be furious.

"I will, but she has unfinished business. Elsa isn't the point. We have a puppet possessed by something evil running loose in town. I think it influenced the arsonist that killed Dixie Campbell last night, then burned Jamie and Graham's house down. We have to stop it, but I don't know where to start. I hoped you would have some insight." I direct the last to my brother.

"I can't help with this. Yes, the puppet was creepy and I grew to hate it, but I don't know what to do about it now. Where is it?"

"That's the point. I don't know where it is or what it wants. I don't even know why whatever is in it is here. I imagine it's been possessed for a long time to get so strong it can run and influence others."

"Is this related to your gift?" Val asks. "Did you get the puppet around that time?" She directs this to Keaton.

"It was later, in the summer," Keaton says. "And how did it get into the puppet to begin with?"

"You're really believing all this?" Cheryl asks Keaton. "This is nuts."

"Lots of things with Rylan are nuts. You just kind of have to go with it," he replies.

This is one of the nicest things he's ever said about me.

"Whether you want to believe me or not, Roland is out there up to who knows what. We have to stop him."

"What does he look like?" Sawyer asks suddenly.

"He's about three feet tall and is dressed like a jester with the colorful clothes and jangle hat. He has blue stars painted over his eyes and a huge red mouth," I say.

"That's right," Keaton says.

Sawyer fishes his phone from his pocket and scrolls. He finally finds what he's looking for and shows us the screen. "Is this him?"

The picture is of a puppet that looks like Roland, but without the air of horror to him. "Where did you get that?"

"I have one of these Roland puppets," Sawyer says, surprising us all. "They were all the rage for a brief time back in the 1920s. I had a time I was into antiques and picked mine up at a flea market a long time ago."

"Yours was named Roland too?" Val asks.

"Yes. They all were. It's the name on the tag."

"So there's more?" I ask with growing fear.

"My puppet is most certainly not possessed. It's just a puppet. It's been put away in my attic for years. I'm sure it's still there."

"When is the last time you saw it?" I ask.

"Not for a long time, but I assure you it's harmless."

"Can you take me to see it?"

THIRTEEN

RYLAN FLYNN

It's nearly dark by the time I pull into Sawyer's driveway behind him. Aunt Val pulls in behind me. I asked Keaton if he wanted to come see the puppet, but he declined. Said he's very familiar with what it looks like already.

As I watch, the front lights flicker on although Sawyer is just now climbing out of his SUV. I hope the sudden lights are not the work of a spirit. I don't get the familiar tingle in my back, so I assume they're on a timer.

The lights make the large house less imposing. Sawyer has done well for himself and has the house to show it, though I prefer Aunt Val's cabin to the mini-mansion.

Sawyer waits for Val and me on the walkway, the last of the sun fading behind him.

"I can't thank you enough for this," I tell him. "I know I ruined your date night. I truly appreciate it."

"Nonsense," Val says. "We can have a date night here just as well."

"Not sure what seeing my Roland will help with, but I'm happy to show him to you."

"I don't know either. But to be honest, I haven't really looked the puppet over very closely. Even before I knew it was haunted, it gave me the creeps. Keaton used to put it in my bed to scare me. I hated the thing." It suddenly dawns on me that Keaton may have been telling the truth back then when he denied putting the puppet in my bed. The thought makes me shiver.

"Let's go," Val says. "I want to see this puppet."

The inside of Sawyer's house is so nicely decorated, I'm fairly certain he had it professionally done. It's too perfect. He leads us through the expansive living room then up the stairs. We walk past bedrooms that look as well appointed as the rest of the house. He stops at a door at the end of the long hall. "The attic is up here," he says, his hand on the knob.

My stomach flutters a bit.

He opens the door and a dark stairway is before us. Sawyer flicks a switch and light pours down the steps.

My belly flips again. I'm not sure why I'm so scared. It's just a toy in an attic. I've faced worse lots of times.

"Right this way," Sawyer says and starts up the steps. Val and I follow close behind.

The attic is a stark contrast to the rest of the house. A haphazard mix of boxes and forgotten items fill the space. There's no apparent plan. It reminds me of my house.

"He's over here," Sawyer says, making his way around a stack of record albums. "At least, I think so. It's been a while."

He moves a box to the side, then opens another.

"Is it in there?" Val asks.

Sawyer reaches into the box and pulls out the identical twin to the thing I've kept locked in Keaton's room.

"Holy flip," I say, stepping back. "That's it."

Sawyer holds the marionette by the back of the neck. Its head hangs to the side.

"I've had this a long time," he says with a touch of nostalgia. "I haven't seen it for a long while."

I suppose, to some, the painted face and outlandish outfit would be whimsical. It scares me.

"Do you know how to do the strings?" Val asks.

"Let's see if I remember how it works." He places the string controller in his hand and the puppet moves jerkily under his control.

I step back, startled. It's too similar to what I saw dancing on my kitchen counter last night.

"There's nothing to worry about," Sawyer says. "He won't hurt you."

"I know," I say. "It's just creepy. It's exactly the same as the other one. Just not possessed or howling at me."

"That must have been awful," Val says, rubbing my arm. "You should have told me. Maybe we could have done something with it."

I think of the big thing I haven't told anyone about – Mom. "I probably should have. But it's not easy to explain. I'm only telling you all now because of the danger."

Sawyer is still making the puppet move and I want to turn my back. I force myself to watch. I wanted to see this one so I would know more about Roland.

"Can you show me how to do that?" I ask. "Is it hard to control?"

"Not too hard, but it takes a little practice." He hands the puppet controller to me. "Here, hold it like this."

I don't want to touch it, but I soon have it moving, albeit not smoothly.

"You're getting it," Val says.

I make the puppet raise its hands and lift its legs. I start to relax, my fear fading. *It's just a toy*, I think. *It can't hurt me.*

I make it bow to Val, and she laughs softly.

The attic lights suddenly go out and the door at the bottom of the steps slams shut.

A different kind of laughter can be heard. The maniacal laughter I need to stop.

FOURTEEN

FORD PIERCE

I can hardly keep my eyes open as I drive home from the police station. It's been a long day after a long night. I barely remember the last time I slept, and I can't wait to get home to my bed.

Tyler, the new detective Faith Hudson and I worked on the case all day. We had the unpleasant task of talking to Dixie's sister in Lafayette. That is always horrible and by far the worst part of this job.

Her cries echo in my ears now. I can only hope they don't haunt my dreams.

The sun is dropping in a bright pink display as I pull into my apartment complex.

"Almost home," I say out loud, taking the familiar turns through the parking lot.

After I park and turn off my car, I sit in the dimness for a moment, too tired to get out.

Thoughts of Rylan sneak their way into my worn mind. What has she done about the puppet today? Should I help her with that? My first priority has to be to Dixie, I know that. What do I make of the text about Travis Cobb? That's twice today his name came up. It has to lead to something. I tried calling and even stopped by his apartment, but I haven't yet made contact. Is that because he's guilty of murder and on the run?

I drag myself from the car and up to my apartment door. As I'm putting my key in the lock, I notice scratches on the painted door. Deep gouges that reveal the metal under the dark blue paint. I bend to touch them, sure they weren't there before. They're about three feet from the ground. It looks like a dog pawed hard at the door.

I'm too tired to care about marks from a dog. I unlock the door and let myself in.

I'm not really hungry, but I know I need to eat, so I fix myself a bowl of cereal and eat it at the counter in the kitchen. Then I crack open a bottle of Miller Lite and drink half of it in one go.

As I'm sitting the bottle down, my phone rings.

I moan loudly. I don't want to answer, but my curiosity is piqued when I see it's Keaton. He may have been my best friend since we were kids, but we rarely get the chance to talk anymore outside of working on a case.

"Hey," I say with as much enthusiasm as I can muster.

"Have you talked to Rylan today?" he asks. Fear courses through me. Is she missing or hurt? Why would Keaton know before me?

"I saw her this morning at the fire."

"Of course she'd have been there," Keaton says. "I guess what I mean is did she tell you anything odd?"

Everything with Rylan is odd, but I think I know what this is about. I pick up my beer and take a long drink, needing it. "Do you mean about that puppet?"

"So she told you. She just told us tonight. Do you think this is real? I don't want to think my sister would make it up, but it's pretty far-fetched."

"It's real. I heard it myself."

A long silence. "I hoped it was a delusion she had," he finally says. "What are we going to do about it?"

"I don't know. I'm kind of covered up with this murder and arson investigation. I don't know how I can help. This is really beyond the scope of police work. I can't go to my chief and tell him about a crazy puppet."

"Yeah, that's what I figured." Keaton sighs. "I should have left it in the dump where I found it. Then we wouldn't be in this mess."

"If it's actually possessed like Rylan thinks, the evil would have just found another thing to take over. The puppet is just what it chose."

"You really think it is evil?"

"I heard it laughing. That didn't sound nice. We recently had a teddy bear that was haunted by a little girl. We released that spirit. This thing may be similar."

"You think it's a ghost, not a demon or something?"

"I can't believe we're having this conversation, but maybe. That's easier to think about than having an evil entity in town."

"None of this is easy," he says.

"No, it isn't." I down the rest of my beer before saying, "Look, there's nothing we can do about it right now. We have no idea where it is or how to stop it. Maybe it's not as dangerous as Rylan thinks. Elsa wasn't dangerous. All I know for sure is I need a few hours' sleep."

"I hear that. Between last night's arrests and today's new murder, we've been swamped too."

"That seems like a lot of murders in a short time," I say, thinking out loud. "Maybe Rylan is onto something. How many bad things can happen in a small town?"

"Let's not find out. You get some rest and we'll talk soon." Keaton says goodbye.

I debate opening another beer, but decide I'd rather have a shower and my bed.

When I finally collapse under the covers, I pull my pillow close.

It smells like Rylan.

FIFTEEN

RYLAN FLYNN

"Wha-what is that horrible sound?" Val asks, stuttering in the dark. "That's it, isn't it? The pu-pu-puppet."

"Yes," I say. "How did it know where to find me?"

"It must be connected to you in some way," Sawyer says.

A tiny sliver of moonlight pierces the shadows through the vent. When I look down, I see Sawyer's puppet, my hand still holding the controller. In shocked reflex, I toss it away. It slams into a box and falls to the floor.

"Holy flip, I'm sorry," I tell Sawyer when I realize I've just thrown a treasured toy across the room.

"It's okay," he says just as the laughing stops. The silence is worse than the laugh. At least when Roland is making noise, we know where he is.

"You think he's still downstairs? Didn't sound like he was up here with us," I say, hoping I'm right. One puppet in this attic is enough.

"Should we go check?" Val asks, grabbing Sawyer's hand. "I don't want to just sit here wondering if it's going to attack."

I listen intently to the dim attic. I don't hear any creaking floor or shuffling sounds. "Let me go. He wants me, not you." I turn on the flashlight on my phone, and pretend to be brave, but inside, I'm quaking.

The light does little to illuminate the huge attic, but I make my way around the stack of albums and a pile of boxes, expecting an ambush at every moment.

I finally reach the steps and look down at the closed door. I stand quietly listening with more than my ears. I don't sense the evil I've grown accustomed to. I only sense an empty attic.

"I don't think he came up," I tell them. "But I don't know where he is or why he came here."

Val and Sawyer round the stack of boxes, their own flash-lights on, and join me by the steps.

"Let's get out of here," Val says and hurries down. She pushes on the door, but it doesn't open. She turns a terrified face up to us. "It's locked."

"This door doesn't have a lock," Sawyer says, hurrying down. "Here, let me." Val steps out of the way and he shoves his shoulder hard into the door.

It opens an inch, then shuts again. "I think he's holding it shut," Sawyer says in surprise. "How is he so strong? Didn't you say you kept him locked in a room for years?" Sawyer slams his shoulder into the door again, this time it barely moves.

"He's growing stronger now that he's out," I say with despair.

"Let's do it together," Val says, joining Sawyer at the door. I slide in next to her. "On the count of three."

In unison, we jam our shoulders into the door. To our surprise, it flies open and we all tumble into the hall. As I catch my balance, I see Roland running down the hall, his strings over his head, controlled by an invisible hand.

"There he goes," I say, running after him without thinking.

"Wait, Rylan," Val calls, but I don't listen.

Roland disappears around the corner in the hall. When I

turn the corner, I no longer see him. In front of me is the wide staircase leading to the first floor.

"Roland?" I call. "I'm coming for you." I start down the steps slowly. Searching below me.

A cackle makes me turn, but not in time.

Strings slide around my neck, then tighten, cutting into my skin.

I feel a weight on my back, pointed feet digging into my shoulders.

I claw at the strings as they pull even tighter.

Aunt Val screams and Sawyer shouts, "Let her go!"

I turn on the steps, afraid I will fall, wanting the thing off me. Roland just pulls the strings more. I see black spots in front of my eyes and try to suck in air. The strings are too tight.

I cling to the railing with one hand, try to yank Roland off with the other.

"Get away!" Sawyer yells and I feel the digging feet leave my shoulders. The strings then unwind from my neck and the puppet flies past my head.

It lands at the bottom of the steps. I expect it to be broken or at least stunned.

Instead, it straightens slowly, the strings taking their place above its head. The huge red mouth drops open and a howl fills the house.

"Make it stop," Val cries.

Coughing after being choked, I take a step down.

Roland suddenly turns and runs across the living room toward the open front door. He disappears into the night, his howl fading as he goes.

"What was that thing?" Aunt Val says. "I mean, I know what it was, but it's so much worse than I thought it would be."

I rub my sore neck and go down the steps to the solid ground of the living room. "I tried to tell you."

"How did you live with that?" Val asks, hurrying down the

steps and taking me into her arms. "Are you okay? Does your neck hurt?"

I don't know which question to answer first, so I just let her hold me.

I start shaking with residual adrenaline. "I thought he had me there for a moment," I say into her shoulder.

"I wasn't going to let that happen," Sawyer says, rubbing my back. "You don't have to fight this thing alone."

"I don't know what we're going to do," I say miserably. "I don't have any ideas. I can't just let it run wild. It's my fault it's here. I have to stop it."

Val pushes me to arm's length and looks at me sharply. "None of this is your fault. Don't talk like that."

"I feel like it's tied to me, and I didn't destroy it."

"Destroying the puppet isn't the answer. You have to cross whatever is inside it," Val says.

My blood runs cold. "I don't think it will cross into the light like the other souls. It doesn't belong there. I don't want to see where it must go."

"You may not have a choice," Sawyer says, shutting the front door and setting the alarm. "But you don't have to do it tonight. Tonight, you can stay here and stay safe."

"The offer sounds wonderful, but I need to go home. I need to check on Elsa." And Mom, I mentally add. "She must be scared."

"What if he comes back to the house?" Val asks full of concern.

"I don't think he will. It's the one place he won't want to return to. The one place that kept him captive."

I start toward the front door. "Seriously, Rylan. Stay here tonight. We can figure all this out in the morning," Val pushes.

"I'll be okay. I promise." I kiss her on the cheek.

"If you're sure," Sawyer says, turning off the alarm again and unlocking the door to let me out.

I look out across his expansive yard, wondering if I'm being a fool for going out into the dark. My neck still stings and my throat is raw from being choked a few minutes ago.

Is this what Ford means when he says I'm reckless?

I really have no choice. If I stay here, Roland will likely come back, and Val and Sawyer might be in danger.

The safest place is for me to be far away from them. The safest place for me is in my house.

I feel Val and Sawyer watching as I hurry down the walkway to my path. I look back as I drive away to see them still in the doorway.

"Lock the door, just in case," I whisper.

Just before I turn the corner, I see them shut the door.

"Rylan's back!" Elsa squeals when I stick my head in the doorway to Mom's room. They're sitting in the dark, so I flip on the light, asking, "Why is the light out? I thought I left it on for you."

"Miss Margie asked me to turn it off," Elsa says with pride.

"I didn't want that horrible thing to see us. I thought maybe we should hide just in case," Mom says.

"I don't think it will come back here," I say. "Probably the last place it will want to come."

"So you didn't catch it?" Elsa asks. "You've been gone so long."

"I stopped by earlier and you two were gone."

Elsa looks stricken.

"It doesn't matter, I'm sorry I was gone for so long, but there's been a lot going on."

"What happened with the fire? Did someone lose their house?" Mom asks.

"The house that burned belongs to Jamie and Graham." I lower my voice. "There was a woman's body inside."

"Oh, how awful," Mom gasps. "Who was she?"

I tell them about talking to Dixie and what happened to her.

"Poor thing," Mom says.

Elsa is unusually subdued. "Another murder?" she asks. "Why do so many people hurt others?"

Mom looks at the girl with concern. "We'll talk more about this later."

"I know it's still pretty early, but I think I'm going to bed. I took a nap at Mickey's, but that feels like a long time ago."

"Why are you rubbing your neck?" Mom asks.

I pull my hand away. I didn't even realize I was doing it.

"I sort of had a run-in with Roland."

Mom's eyes narrow as she crosses the room to study my neck. "You have marks here. What happened?"

I sigh heavily and tell her about what happened at Sawyer's.

"Oh, Rylan, I don't like any of this," she says. "Why do you always have to be the one in harm's way?"

"You sound like Ford," I say, leaning against the door jamb.

"That's because we both love you and want you safe. You should listen to that boy."

"If we were still together, maybe I would."

"That will blow over in no time." She waves a hand. "You just have to stop being so stubborn."

"Maybe he needs to stop being so controlling," I counter.

"Maybe you two are just so afraid of your feelings you're looking for a reason to mess this up."

She has me there. "I have too much going on to worry about my love life right now."

"I like Ford. You should marry him," Elsa pops into the conversation, making both Mom and me laugh.

"It's not that easy," I sigh.

"Then you could have a baby," she adds. "I could help you take care of it."

"I think this conversation has gotten a little off track," I say, smiling at the girl's enthusiasm.

"I always wanted Mommy to have another baby, but she said I was all she needed." She suddenly turns sad. "Will I ever see Mommy again?"

The energy in the room suddenly dips. "I don't know, honey. I've tried to talk to her, but she doesn't believe in ghosts and sent me away."

"Maybe I can talk to her and then she'll believe."

I don't see that happening, but I say, "Maybe."

"You should get some sleep," Mom says, sitting back on the bed.

"Good night," I say and turn back to the hall.

Only then do I remember the door to Keaton's room is still hanging open. The light from the hall shines in on a few of the crosses covering the walls.

On impulse, I step inside and the crosses surround me. What was meant to trap Roland comforts me now.

I drop to my knees in the middle of the room and bow my head.

"Lord, please help me stop him," I whisper the simple words full of feeling over and over.

A peaceful feeling warms me from the inside. After a long moment, I open my eyes and stand up.

"Amen," I say as I leave the room, carefully closing the door behind me.

SIXTEEN

KEATON FLYNN

Of all the strange evenings I've had where my sister is concerned, this is definitely the strangest. I originally didn't want to get involved, but this is different than a typical ghost sighting. This is partially my fault. I brought the puppet home.

I dart a glance at Cheryl once we get home and settle on our black leather couch. Does all this nonsense about a possessed puppet bother her? She's known for a while that me having a sister that sees and talks to ghosts can be a challenge, but this is a bit beyond that.

"Why do you keep looking at me like that?" she finally asks, muting the show on TV.

"I was just wondering how you felt about all this puppet stuff."

"Well, it's not something I expected to hear tonight, but when it comes to Rylan, I don't suppose I should be too surprised. You don't think this is real, do you? I know you said as much to Ford, but do you really believe?"

"Rylan wouldn't make this up."

"Would she, though?" she asks. "The ghost stuff is enough

of a stretch. Is there really some possessed puppet traipsing around town right now?"

"That's not fair." I'm surprised at the defensiveness I feel. Haven't I had the same thoughts about what Rylan does? "Imagine living with that thing like she has. I, personally, like the puppet. It was creepy-looking and what teenage boy doesn't like that? But I haven't thought about it since I moved out years ago."

"You had no idea something was wrong with it?"

"Not really," I say, but I know that's not true. There were a few times when I'd woken to strange laughter, barely audible, coming from the dark. That had really scared me although I would never tell anyone about it. To my young mind, it only made it cooler.

Cheryl takes a long moment to respond. Then she turns on the couch and meets my eyes. "So, what are we going to do about it?"

"I have no idea," I tell her honestly.

"Here's what I'm thinking." She's growing animated. "If the evil in the puppet has been with Rylan all this time, it makes sense that it's attached to her in some way."

"Okay?" I ask, not sure I like where this might head.

"And to catch him, we need bait."

"You want to use Rylan as bait for a demented puppet?"

"We'd be there to help. We wouldn't let her get hurt," she tries to assure me.

"No way. Rylan and I might have our issues, but I'm not going to put her in danger on purpose." I know Cheryl is just trying to help, but I don't like this.

"She wouldn't actually be in danger. I mean, what can a puppet do to you anyway?"

"Influence others to do awful things for one." I stare at her harshly. Is she under the influence a little?

"Don't look at me like that," she snaps. "I'm just trying to help."

"That isn't helpful." I sit back against the couch cushion, stare at the muted TV; a dog food commercial plays. The perfect world depicted there seems far away from this conversation.

"Do you have any other ideas?" she pushes.

"No. But I will." We sit in uncomfortable silence, staring at the TV until the commercials give way to the news. I turn up the volume. The lead story is about the murder and arson.

"Do you think that is tied to the puppet?" Cheryl asks.

"Maybe. Ford and Tyler interviewed a few suspects today. Nothing has stuck."

"So they have nothing?"

"Not nothing. These things take time and a lot of legwork. They have a good suspect, but get this." I know I shouldn't be talking about the case, but the connection is bothering me, and I'd like her take on it.

"What?"

"The suspect is a friend of Rylan's."

A long moment passes while she thinks this over. "Everything comes back to your sister one way or another," she finally says. "Don't you think that's weird?"

"I do. It's always ghosts this or ghosts that. I heard she even saw the ghost of the victim in that fire." I'm surprised at the heat in my words. "She's at the center of all the crimes recently."

"Curious," Cheryl says.

One word. One heavy word.

I don't like the path my mind is going down, but Rylan did live with the puppet that she herself said is possessed and influences others. "Yes, it is curious."

SEVENTEEN

The burning heats my soul, the ever-present urge to destroy him.

I'll never forgive and I'll never forget.

The savagery in my mind almost scares me. Almost.

I look at the picture on my phone: a face I've memorized.

I know where to find him, know what must be done. They are connected. It's perfect.

A scratching on my window stops the reverie. Slowly, I approach the glass and peer into the darkness.

Starred eyes stare back at me, a red mouth hanging open. The face I've seen in my dreams. I open the window, and the thing climbs into the room the way it has climbed into my soul.

EIGHTEEN

RYLAN FLYNN

I doze in my bed, tired, but tossing. Onyx the cat had been lying near me, but after all my moving around, he took off. The room is still clean from my recent purge of the mess. Usually, when I'm fully awake, I like the new space.

Now, though, I miss the clutter, the protective barrier.

I don't think Roland will come back, but I'm not sure.

I rub at my neck, still stinging from the tight puppet strings he strangled me with. What if Sawyer hadn't knocked him away? Would the thing finally kill me? Is that the game we're playing? Cat and mouse with me on the losing end.

I don't intend to lose.

Flipping onto my side, I push a pillow against my face, but it doesn't block the thoughts swirling in my mind. When my phone rings, I'm happy for the distraction.

The emotion turns to worry when I see it's Mickey calling. Visions of puppet strings around her neck emerge.

"Everything okay?" I ask instead of saying hello.

"Hey. Yeah, we're fine. Except, someone needs you."

My tired mind doesn't quite follow the cryptic words. "Who?"

"I was just checking our email before I went to bed, and I found a message from a security guard at the courthouse. He said to tell you the lady in red is throwing things and to please come right away. Do you know what that means?"

I sit up in bed and swing my legs over the side. "I do. Can you meet me at the courthouse with the camera?"

"Now?"

"How long ago did the email come in?" I pull on my skinny jeans and look for my Chuck Taylors.

"About half an hour ago. You're really going now?"

"Stan and I've been talking about the lady. He said she was getting restless. If she's making such a ruckus that Stan emailed us, it must be bad."

"I'll be right there."

I grab my leather jacket and run a hand through my hair. "I'm going out," I shout into Mom's room, but when I look in, it's empty. I don't have time to worry about what Mom and Elsa might be up to now.

I beat Mickey to the courthouse. The square is lit up by streetlights and floodlights shine up on the limestone walls of the Greek Revival-style building. It's lovely in the night.

I wait for Mickey at the base of the steps. A few cars drive past the square, but the night is peaceful. If it wasn't for the tingling in my lower back, I'd enjoy the moment. Instead, I give myself a pep talk and pace. After my run-in with Roland earlier, I'm a bit spooked and I'm not even facing a ghost yet.

After a few minutes, Mickey parks next to my car and then joins me with her camera in hand.

"Ready?" I ask without preamble, turning up the steps.

"Are you going to tell me what this is about?"

"Let's see what Stan has to say first, and I'll fill in the blanks after that." I reach for the glass door, but it opens before I can pull it.

"You came," Stan says, letting us in.

"You said it was urgent," Mickey says. "So I called Rylan right away." Stan looks pointedly at the camera. "I'm Mickey. Rylan's partner and cameraperson."

"You're going to film this?" he asks, full of worry.

"Is that okay? I film most of my encounters for the show."

"Right, of course, of course." He ushers us past the security check-in and into the dark lobby. In the distance, glass breaks. "She's very upset and is breaking things all over. Bart, the night guard, saw a book fly into a display case and he freaked out and called me. I knew right away what was going on. By the time I got here, Bart had already high-tailed it out."

Something tumbles down the stairway and lands at our feet. It's the bust of Aristotle, the nose now broken off and part of his neck missing. "She's strong tonight. That thing has to weigh several pounds," I say, impressed.

Mickey turns on her camera and gets a shot of the marble head. When she focuses the camera on me, I introduce myself and give a short rundown of what I know about the lady. Beyond what she looks like, I don't have any information. Normally, I'll do at least some cursory research before going to a haunting so I know what I'm getting into. I should have done that when Stan first told me about a spirit here. No time for that now.

A wild scream echoes through the lobby. For a terrified moment, I think it's Roland.

"You hear that?" I ask Stan.

He glances at the camera, then back at me. "I don't think so. What do you hear?"

"Screaming. Come on." I hurry up the steps wrapping around the lobby toward the sound.

The second floor is illuminated only by small night lights

near the floor. The floor is littered with books and broken glass. We step around the mess. The screaming stops, but we turn down the hall where it was coming from. At the end of the hall, glowing brightly and singing to herself, stands the lady in red. Her 1920s dress is torn in front and her face is bruised. It looks like she's been crying.

"Hello?" I say gently. "Are you okay?"

She looks up sharply. Her eyes widen when she realizes I'm talking to her. "You're the one that can see me, aren't you?"

"My name is Rylan. What's yours?"

"I'm Jean. Did that security guard tell you to come talk to me?" Jean motions to Stan. "He gets scared easily. Not as easily as the one that works here at night, though."

I repeat this for the camera.

"Why do you want to scare them?"

She shrugs her mostly bare shoulder. "I'm bored. It's so lonely here all alone. Sure, there are people in and out all day, but no one hears me or sees me. No one talks to me."

"I bet it's hard to be alone all the time. Tell me, Jean, do you know why you're here and not crossed over?"

"You mean crossed into heaven?" she asks with disbelief. "I gave up believing in heaven a long time ago."

"It's real. I've helped many spirits cross."

She twirls a loose curl and thinks on this. "You could help me?"

"If that's what you want."

"Then do it. Right now. I'm ready."

"It's not that easy. Only God decides when you're ready. I just ask for His help."

"So ask. What are you waiting for?"

"It's been my experience that spirits like you are waiting to cross for a reason. Do you know what the reason might be?" I ask.

"If I did, I'd have done it by now, wouldn't I?" Jean snaps.

I raise my hands in supplication. "Okay. I get it. Let's start at the beginning. Are you from Ashby?"

"Unfortunately. I always wanted to move to the city, but I'm born and raised here and never escaped."

"And then you've been captive here in the courthouse for a century judging by your dress."

Jean looks down at her torn red dress. "This thing? Not my favorite dress and I get stuck with it for all this time. Red is not my color. I'm more of a blue girl. Brings out my eyes."

"I'm sure it does. If you don't like the dress, what were you wearing it for? A special occasion?"

"My husband gave it to me as a gift, so I thought I better wear it. It was an important night, and he said I had to look good for a change. He was winning the Man of the Year award at a banquet they held here. He was a bigwig on the city council." She says this with disgust. "Man of the Year, sure. More like creep of the year, but no one knew that but me."

I repeat all this for the camera and go on. "Did something happen at the dinner?"

"Not during dinner, but during his speech after they presented the award. I may have accidentally laughed a little as he was speaking. I swear, I didn't mean to. It just slipped out."

"That had to make him mad," I push. "Did he hurt you?"

"He invited me for a walk up here on the second floor. You know all those display cases by the stairway? They had artwork in them back then. He said he wanted to show the art to me." She looks at the floor. "I thought he was being romantic for a change and I felt bad about laughing, so I went."

"What happened?"

"It was late. Most people had already left and we were all alone up here. He started yelling at me the way he always did. I didn't pay him much attention. He was always harping at me over something. This made him more mad. He eventually grabbed me by the dress and pushed me up against the railing that overlooks the lobby. I didn't think he'd actually hurt me, but I was nervous."

As she talks, she moves toward the banister until her hands rest on it.

I tell the story to the camera, then ask, "What happened?"

Her voice sounds far away. "He pushed me."

I give her a moment, then continue. "And you've been here ever since?"

She seems to come back to herself and turns to face me. "I have. It's only one story to the floor, but I landed on my head and died instantly. Dying was bad enough, but he told everyone that I jumped. I would never do that. My poor family was devastated. My father came to this very spot and told me I had disgraced the Flynn family. He didn't know I could hear him, of course, but the words stung just the same."

I swallow hard. "Did you say Flynn family? Is that your last name?"

"Why sure. Jean Flynn was my maiden name."

NINETEEN
RYLAN FLYNN

I repeat what she said for the camera, then look to Mickey for her reaction. She peeks around the camera, her eyes wide.

"Small world," Stan says. "You two must be relatives."

Jean stares at me. "You're a Flynn too?"

"I am."

"Huh." She pushes a stray curl out of her face. "I didn't have any children, but my older brother had several."

"Was your brother's name Brett?"

"It was," Jean says with obvious pride.

"That must be my great-great-grandpa. My dad was named after him."

"That makes me your aunt. Now do your old auntie a favor and get me out of here."

"I told you, it doesn't work like that, but I can try."

I'm conscious of the camera and Stan watching me. I don't want to let anyone down, but something tells me Jean isn't ready to cross yet and no amount of prayer can open the light. "First, I will say some prayers, then we hope the passage opens."

Jean smacks her hands together. "Great. I'm ready. Get to praying."

I do my best to remember the prayers Dad always says. I ad-lib a bit, but I think I do a pretty good job of trying to lead her soul to heaven.

Nothing happens.

"Why isn't it working?" Jean asks. "I don't see anything."

"It only works if whatever you are here for is taken care of. At least that's the way I understand it. Is there anything else that might be keeping you on this side? Something unresolved?"

"Everyone I ever knew has passed away. My husband died years ago with no one the wiser that he was a murderer. What could be left?"

I don't know how to respond to that. What could be left? I can't get her justice. Her husband has met his maker and has been dealt with in the hereafter.

I turn to face the camera, but before I can say anything, I see Lindy Parker hurrying toward us down the hall.

"What in the world are you all doing in here?" she demands. She focuses her venom on Stan. "You let them in?"

"I, there's—" he stammers.

"What are you doing here this late?" I counter.

"I was working, unlike you," she snides.

"I am working. There's a spirit here that I'm helping."

Lindy shakes her head in disgust. "Sure there is. You two still peddling that song and dance about crossing souls? I thought you'd outgrow that eventually."

"Tell her I'm real," Jean says. "Tell her."

"Why don't you just leave us alone? I'm not hurting you, but I'm helping Jean," I say.

"Jean? You gave your imaginary friend a name?"

"She's not imaginary."

"I'm real!" Jean shouts at the same time.

Only then does Lindy realize this whole interaction is being filmed. "And get that camera out of here." She reaches for the lens and Mickey steps back.

"Okay, now, Ms. Parker. That's enough. I let them in. You are free to leave," Stan says.

"Oh, I'll leave. Wait until I tell your brother." Lindy turns on her sensible heel and starts toward the stairs. "What is this mess?" she asks about the smashed display cases, stopping.

"The ghost did it," Stan says. "She's mad about being murdered."

Lindy puts a hand on her hip. "And now she's a murder victim. You really are something, Rylan. Don't we have enough problems today with the homicide and arson case? Do you have to make stuff up for fun?"

"I did not make it up!" Jean shouts and rushes toward Lindy. I brace for the impact, but Jean simply passes right through her. Lindy doesn't even notice. She just shakes her head at us and starts down the steps.

Jean picks up a small statue from the display case and throws it at Lindy. It hits her in the back.

Lindy freezes, then turns slowly on the second step. "Did you just throw that at me?"

"Jean did," I say.

"Sure. The ghost threw it."

Jean picks up another statue from the display case and throws this one too, yelling, "I'll show you I'm real."

The small statue hits Lindy in the chest. "What in the world? How did you do that?"

"Jean is mad that you don't believe in her. I told you she's real. Now you know."

Lindy walks back up the steps, her eyes wide with shock. "Make her do it again."

I don't have to ask her. Jean grabs an old book that lies on the floor and throws it against a wall.

"What?" Lindy asks in shock.

"That's why I emailed Rylan," Stan says. "The ghost is

breaking things and making a mess. I didn't know what else to do."

"You have to stop this," Lindy says to me. "Do whatever you do, but make her stop breaking things."

"I already tried to cross her over, but there's something keeping her here."

"Like what?"

"I have no idea. She said she's a Flynn. Brett Flynn was her brother and my father is named after him, his great-grandfather. That's the only real revelation we've had."

"Besides murder," Jean says. "I finally got to tell my story. Isn't that enough to move on?"

Lindy is chewing on her lip, thinking. "You say Brett Flynn is your great-great-grandfather?"

"That's right. Why?"

"I did some genealogy when I was in college. My great-great-grandmother's brother was a Brett Flynn."

"That would be Samantha, my baby sister. She must have had kids after I was killed. It's like a family reunion around here," Jean says.

My mood sinks. "Is that grandmother Samantha Flynn?" I ask Lindy.

Her eyes narrow in distrust. "Yes. That was her maiden name. She married Jonas Parker."

"Jean says that's her little sister. Looks like we're all related."

"I had hoped it was just a fluke. Lots of people have the same name. I don't want to be related to you." Her harsh honesty stings a little.

"I'm so sorry to disappoint you," I say with heavy sarcasm.

"I didn't mean it like that."

"Okay, ladies, let's not get too excited here," Stan says. "That was a long time ago. Besides, you can't choose your family."

"Just think, two of my great-nieces here at once," Jean beams. "And I brought you together."

"She's excited to have us both here," I tell everyone and the camera.

"Is that what I was waiting for?" Jean asks. "To tell the truth about what happened to me and to know that my family lived on despite my death?"

"Maybe," I say, then repeat what she said for the camera.

"So the Keaton Flynn that works here is my nephew?" Jean asks.

"He's my brother."

"Interesting. Are there others? Other family I don't know?"

"Let's see. My dad of course, and Aunt Val, his sister."

"Can you bring them here? I want to see them. What about her?" She points to Lindy.

"She wants to meet your family," I tell Lindy. "Can you bring them here?"

"No way. I'm not telling them anything about this. They will not believe in ghosts. I don't really believe either. I feel like I'm in some strange dream right now."

"No dream. Just a soul looking for some peace," I tell her.

"That's your area," Lindy says. "I don't want anything to do with it." She starts down the stairs again. "I'm going home and having a glass of wine. This is nuts, even for you."

"It's not nuts," I say, defensive.

"And Stan," she continues. "You're lucky if I don't have your job for this. Be sure to clean up all this glass and mess before you go."

"Yes, Ms. Parker."

"Now what?" Jean asks once Lindy is gone.

"I guess I'll bring Dad and Val to see you. Maybe then you can cross. Dad will help. He helps me a lot. He's a pastor."

"A pastor in the family. That's wonderful."

"He is pretty wonderful, yes. I will talk to them and see if they can come tomorrow night. Will that work?"

"I've waited a hundred years. Another night won't make any difference." Jean floats over the broken glass. "Sorry about the mess," she says to Stan although he can't hear her. "I was just upset."

I tell Stan what she said.

"No worries, Miss Jean. I will clean it up."

Jean is headed down the steps when she grabs her chest and gasps. "Did you see that?" she asks me.

I join her on the steps, looking into the lobby. "See what?"

What could scare a ghost?

"I swear I just saw a puppet run across the lobby."

My stomach sinks and I run down the steps, shouting, "Roland," into the dimness. The lobby is empty, but several halls branch off of it. If Roland is here, he could have gone down any of them.

"Why are you calling my husband's name?" Jean asks, joining me in the lobby.

"It's a long story, but I'm calling after a possessed marionette named Roland. Was that your husband's name?"

"Yes." Jean begins twirling her hair in thought. "That's strange. My Roland had a marionette puppet. His brother bought it for him sort of like a joke. The puppet's name was Roland, too, and they thought it was funny. I swear what I just saw looks exactly like the one we had."

I let this all sink in. "I recently learned that the puppet was fairly popular back in the 1920s, but what are the odds that there are three of them? This one must be your husband's."

The horrible laughter echoes down a hall, growing closer as the puppet runs toward us. It stops in front of Jean and me, lifts its horrible head. "Hello, Jeanie Bean." It snarls.

Jean gasps and jumps back. "Roland?"

"Good to see you again," he hisses, reaching a hand for her.

"Get away from me," she yells, terrified.

A flash of blue as Stan kicks at the puppet. Roland slides across the lobby floor, regains his feet and runs out the front door.

"What in the world?" Mickey says, joining us, the camera on her shoulder. "I recorded the whole thing. That's what you were telling me about?"

"Yes." My breath is tight in my chest.

"What an awful thing," Mickey says.

"I thought it was going for you, Rylan," Stan says.

"He was reaching for Jean."

Jean is pale and unusually quiet. "That's him," she says in a low voice. "That was my husband. He always called me Jeanie Bean. I hated the nickname, but he insisted."

"The puppet is your husband?" I ask, pieces clicking into place.

"I think so." She nods. "I don't want to stay here, I want you to cross me. Please, if Roland is in that puppet of his, then I'm not safe. He'll come back to hurt me."

"You're a ghost. There's nothing he can do to you now," I say gently. "Besides, you can't cross until you resolve what you need to resolve."

"What is that?" she asks.

"It may be to see your family. I'll bring Dad and Val and even Keaton maybe tomorrow night and we'll try again. Until then, stay hidden in case Roland comes back."

"You don't have to ask me twice," she says and promptly disappears.

"She's gone," I say. "What a wild encounter."

Mickey says, "You're not kidding. This was wild, even for us. A possessed puppet attacks a ghost. Never thought I'd see that. And just imagine, you and Lindy are cousins."

"Distant, distant cousins," I point out. "Not really related in my book."

"Still interesting."

I push some broken glass that fell into the lobby with the toe of my sneaker. "Let's just get this glass cleaned up so we can go home."

"You don't have to help," Stan says. "You've helped enough for one night. I can sweep this up. Of course, I don't know what to say about the broken displays."

"I don't suppose the truth will go over well at a government building," Mickey says.

"Not so much," he agrees. "But there are security cameras covering the whole place. If anyone besides me and Bart see the footage that could get complicated. But I'll deal with it."

"Well, good luck," I tell him earnestly. "I wish we could help more. At least Jean should behave until we come back tomorrow night. Will you be able to get us in again?"

"I can arrange it with Bart. I'm sure he won't want to work another night shift for a while."

"Great. See you then." Mickey and I descend the wide steps into the lobby. The courthouse is almost peaceful now that Jean has disappeared. "I'll be back," I call into the dimness, just in case Jean can hear me.

Out on the sidewalk, I ask Mickey, "You headed home?"

"Marco wasn't too pleased that I left. I better get back."

I don't like that her husband is once again against us doing our work, but I hold my tongue.

"Did you have something in mind?" she asks.

"After all that's happened, I could really use a drink. I was thinking of stopping by The Lock Up before trying to sleep."

A flicker of some emotion crosses her face, but disappears before I can recognize it. Was it fear?

"I'm sorry. I can't. Like I said."

"I understand." But I really don't. I try not to let the hurt show. I give her a quick hug, then say, "Catch you later," and get in the Cadillac.

I mull over the encounter with Jean as I drive to The Lock Up. I know I should go home, but one vodka tonic won't hurt and it might help me unwind.

When I pull into the parking lot, I see a truck I recognize from this morning.

Fire Chief Aiden Andrews is here.

TWENTY

RYLAN FLYNN

I almost turn out of the parking lot without going in. Then I tell myself not to be silly. I just faced down a ghost and a possessed puppet, a man should be easy.

Besides, it's not like we came here together. I might not even run into him.

"Just a quick drink," I say as I walk across the gravel parking lot. I can almost taste the slightly bitter tonic already.

It's not too crowded and there's an open seat near the waitress station at the bar. I slide onto the plastic stool and wait for the bartender to see me. Luckily, it's a man tonight, not the blonde woman that is often here.

The huge mirror behind the bar gives me a good view of the room. I see a few people that look familiar, but no one pays me any attention. Just the way I like it. I'm not looking for him, but I spot Aiden at a corner table with a few other men. They're having a lively discussion about something.

He must have felt me looking because he glances my way and meets my eyes in the mirror.

I look away and feel my face flush. I'd hoped he wouldn't see me. I'd rather be here with Ford.

Maybe coming here was a mistake. Just as I'm about to slide out of my seat and leave, the bartender approaches with a friendly smile. "What can I get ya?" he says, sliding a napkin my way.

I don't want to be rude. "Vodka tonic with lime," I say and settle back onto the stool. One quick drink and I'm out of here.

"Put that on our tab." Aiden is suddenly at my shoulder. "Rylan Flynn. What a lovely surprise."

Caught, I turn in my seat. "Hey," I say lamely.

"Been out ghost hunting?" he asks. For a moment, I think he found out about the courthouse, but I realize he's just talking generally.

"Just on my way home," I say as the bartender hands me my drink.

"I'm glad to see you," he says. "We aren't staying long either. A few of the off-duty guys asked me to come out with them. I thought it might be good for morale to come along."

"I see," I say, then take a big sip on my straw, the tonic sliding across my tongue and the vodka warming my belly. I take another sip, but this one goes down the wrong way.

I choke on the drink.

Aiden pats me on the back as I gasp to regain control.

"Careful there," he says.

I want to disappear into the floor. "I'm okay," I mutter, my eyes watering.

His hand remains on my back in what could be a friendly manner. I don't want it, but fight the urge to shake him off.

Instead, I turn in my chair to face him, forcing him to remove his hand.

"We didn't get to talk this morning before we were interrupted. I'd still like to hear all about your show."

I'm tired and don't really want to talk about work right now. I don't want to talk at all. I just want to drink my drink in peace.

"Sure, sometime." I turn back to face the bar, hoping he'll get the hint and return to his table.

Instead, he leans on the bar. "I got time now."

I don't want to be rude. I really don't. He's the fire chief and deserves respect, but I'm not interested. I open my mouth to say something along those lines, but his phone goes off before I can get the words out.

"I'm sorry," he says, looking at the phone, reading something. "Looks like duty calls." He waves for the bartender. "I'll close the tab now."

As the bartender takes his card, he says, "Big fire over on Elm. You should come."

I'm surprised at the invitation.

"Why me?"

"They found another body in the fire. Maybe you can help."

I slide my half-full glass to the inside of the bar and say, "I'll meet you there."

Aiden's truck is equipped with lights so he can get to the fire quickly. I follow close behind, sliding through red lights and stop signs with him. It's not strictly legal, but he did ask me to come to the scene.

Besides, I want to get there as fast as possible in case the victim's spirit is still around for me to talk to.

As we pull into the scene, I drop back and park down the block. As I walk to the burned house, I don't get a tingle in my back of a spirit close by. Still, I search the dark and all the people milling about.

The dark is empty and the people are all of the living. I join the gathering crowd and watch the flames lick the sky. The nearly full moon shines through the smoke, making a scary scene even more eerie. I feel the heat of the fire on my cheeks and the smoke burns my eyes.

I should move back or leave.

But I'm held to my spot. I need to be here even if there are no ghosts to talk to.

The crew works feverishly and soon the fire is out, but half the house is lost. The other half sags precariously.

Two firefighters in full gear exit what remains of the house, each holding the end of a tarp with a sheet over it.

They've removed the body already.

I watch as they set it down carefully, no doubt waiting for the coroner. A uniformed officer is putting up yellow tape, now that they know it's a crime scene. It's Officer James Frazier. His eyes narrow when he sees me.

I look away, but he approaches.

"Seriously?" he asks. "Do you think we can't do our work without you here to watch?"

"I was invited," I say stiffly.

"The detectives aren't here yet."

"It wasn't Ford that invited me." I look across the busy yard to Aiden. Frazier follows my gaze.

"Oh, so that's how it is. Didn't take you long," he says with disgust.

"It's not like that," I start to defend myself. Frazier just walks away without listening, rolling the yellow tape between us.

He waits for me to step back, making sure I'm on the outside.

Maybe I should leave. I don't feel any spirits nearby, so I can't help in that way. But I'm worried about Roland showing himself again. It can't be coincidence that he's loose and there's another fire and a victim. He has to be involved somehow.

I wish I could stop him. But even if I catch him, what then? I don't think Keaton's room will contain him now, regardless of how many crosses I hang.

The wind picks up, blowing smoke in my face and chilling me. I wrap my leather jacket closer.

I really should go. Aiden is busy and Ford will be here any minute. He'll be about as happy as Frazier was to see me. Not to mention the coroner is for sure on his way too.

I turn to head back to my car, but find Ford standing behind me.

My heart skips a beat as we stare at each other. I can't make out his expression in the shadows. I don't think it's a smile, though.

"You should be home in bed," he says, not unkindly, taking a step closer.

"I was in bed. Then I got called out on a job." I don't know how to explain my presence here, so I skip over that part. "They just brought out a body."

Ford looks past me to the scene. "Yeah. That's what I was told," he says somberly.

"I need to stop this. I'm sure the puppet has some part in all of it. I should never have let him escape."

"Whatever is going on here started long before it got out."

"It's still my responsibility."

He studies me for a long moment. "You're always so concerned with everyone else," he says with a touch of admiration.

I grow warm at the praise. "I try."

"You need to take care of yourself too." I bristle at this and he notices. "I'm not telling you what to do. I know you'll do what you need." He runs a hand over his face. "Just be careful, okay?" A plea I can't disregard.

"I will," I respond, breathless.

His eyes are soft and his hand reaches for my hair, then he suddenly hardens and drops his arm.

"Pierce, you made it," Aiden says behind me. "Rylan, did you sense anything this time?"

"No. Nothing. I'm sorry," I say to Aiden as Ford dips under the yellow tape and walks away, the tender moment completely ruined.

TWENTY-ONE
FORD PIERCE

I walk away from Rylan and Aiden Andrews. I know I have to work with him, but I don't have to like it. What game is he playing with her anyway?

I shrug my shoulders and remind myself that it isn't my business anymore. I broke up with her. She's free to do what she wants.

But I know I'm just attempting to fool myself. I can feel her eyes on my back. When I glance over my shoulder, she's talking to Andrews but watching me.

That's a good sign, right?

I need to focus. The person under the sheet deserves my full attention. Tyler arrives and joins me by the body, and I turn my attention to him.

"Another one, huh?" he says mostly to himself.

"Has to be related to last night's. It's possible this victim lives here and this is just an accident, but that would be a huge coincidence," I say.

"Right," he says. "So, what have we got? I see they brought the body out already." Tyler studies what's left of the house.

Part of the remaining roof falls as we watch, making me jump back.

"Glad they did," I say. "That is dangerous."

"Do we know whose house this is?" Tyler asks.

"I got here just before you did. I talked to Rylan, then you pulled up."

"Rylan's here? Did she learn anything?" he asks, full of hope.

"No," I answer curtly.

"Okay, then. I see you two haven't made up yet."

"Let's just focus on the job." I crouch next to the body and lift the corner of the sheet.

"We should wait for Faith."

"They called her in already?" I ask, standing again.

"Direct from the chief as I understand it."

Waiting for Faith gives me time to glance over at Rylan. She's standing alone on the other side of the tape. Andrews is talking to his men. I know she knows I'm watching her, but she looks at the ground.

Damn, she's beautiful.

I shove that thought far away and am happy to see Faith Hudson arrive.

"Hey," she says. Faith and Tyler have worked together, but, until today, I haven't paid her any attention. She seems capable enough and I'm happy for the help. This case is quickly getting out of hand.

The facts point to Graham Rock as our suspect, but this new case might change all that.

"Do we know whose house this is?" Faith asks.

I hadn't given it any thought and I should have. I mentally chastise myself as Tyler answers, "I think it's the house flippers, Jamie and Graham's still. This doesn't look good for him."

"How do you know that?" I ask.

"This is the house where Jamie found that body on that case a while back," Tyler says.

I study what's left of the house. It was once a two-story with a porch, much like most of the houses in this neighborhood. I didn't recognize it, but Tyler is right. The house belongs to Graham Rock.

"This has to be enough to bring him in," Faith says.

"It may be," I say. "But first we need to find out who is under this sheet," I say, crouching again.

I hesitate with the corner of the sheet in my fingers. Burned bodies are horrible. Tyler and I just saw one less than twenty-four hours ago. I doubt Faith has ever seen one.

"You ready?" I ask her. "It's pretty bad."

She pushes one of her long braids behind an ear. "I'm ready."

I slide the sheet back and the charred remains are revealed. It's hard to determine anything from the blackened corpse. Slight of build and not excessively tall, it's either a small man or a woman. A tiny amount of skin remains and appears to be Caucasian. Even the hair is singed off. It could be anyone.

"Phew," Faith says, bending closer to the body. "There really isn't much to go on."

"Is that a gold tooth?" Tyler asks, pointing to where the lips are pulled back from the teeth.

"It is. That should narrow it down a bit, but not much," I say.

"We just have to figure out who Graham Rock wanted hurt and also has a gold tooth," Faith says, standing tall and brushing her hands on her pants.

I know she's right, but something is niggling at me. "It's too easy," I say, standing straight.

"The easy answer is often the correct one," Tyler says.

"True. But maybe we are looking at this wrong. Two people own both houses."

"You think Jamie did this?" Tyler asks.

"I think it's possible. I just don't want to run to the DA with this and be wrong."

"Or we run and get him off the street before he burns another innocent person," Faith says.

"Good way to look at it too. Let's not rush it," I say. "What do you think?" I look to Tyler for his reaction. He's watching the scene techs ducking under the tape, his eye on one in particular.

"You going to ask her out tonight?" I say.

He seems surprised at the question. "I don't think it's right. This is a crime scene and all."

"Ask her out," Faith says. "I can tell by the way she's looking at you that she'll say yes."

"We went for coffee once," Tyler says.

"Coffee doesn't mean anything," I say too quickly.

"Dinner. Ask her to dinner. Maybe a drink after," Faith says. "Life's short and Marrero is still at the van."

She's right, the coroner hasn't entered the scene yet. If Tyler is going to make a move, it's now.

He doesn't need any more prompting from us, he just strides up to Michelle and starts talking. I'm impressed he finally got up the nerve, and judging by the way she's smiling, she's accepting the invitation.

Almost of their own will, my eyes search for Rylan. She's still standing beyond the yellow tape on the sidewalk. Faith is right. Life is short.

I cross the yard to her, noticing how her eyes widen at my approach.

"I hoped you were still here," I say because I don't know what else to say.

"I'm waiting to see if I can be of some help. Besides, this is Jamie and Graham's house. They're on their way."

I'm not surprised she remembered the house, even when I didn't.

"Look," I start, not sure how I will finish the sentence. "I think we need to talk."

The breeze blows a strand of her long brown hair toward me. I want to take it in my fingers, want to pull her close.

"This isn't the place," she says, breaking the spell she had me under. "Marrero is glaring at us."

Right now, I don't care about Marrero and his crankiness. I don't care that the whole fire department and most of the police department can see.

All I care about is this woman in front of me.

I open my mouth to tell her that I was wrong, but she cuts me off. "Later," she says a touch breathlessly. "We'll talk later. Right now, you need to catch this killer because I know it looks bad for Graham and Jamie, but I assure you they are innocent."

The case. She's right. What was I thinking?

"How can you be so sure?" I ask.

"I trust my friends."

"Do you trust me?" I didn't mean to say that, but now that I have, I want to hear her answer.

"I did until you broke up with me." Do I hear a catch in her voice?

"Pierce, is now good for you for an investigation?" Marrero calls across the yard as he moves toward the body. "I don't know what's gotten into you detectives tonight," he grumbles.

"The body has a gold tooth," I tell Rylan. "Does that mean anything to you?" I ask as I start back across the yard.

"I don't think so, but I'll ask Jamie and Graham when they get here."

I should be the one to ask them. I shouldn't even have told Rylan about it.

What's wrong with me tonight?

TWENTY-TWO

RYLAN FLYNN

I wish my back would start tingling. Wish I could talk to the victim with a gold tooth. There's a tingle low in my belly, but it has nothing to do with spirits and everything to do with the man I can't seem to keep my eyes off.

Despite our current situation, Ford Pierce will always hold my attention. He always has. He may be frustrating me to no end, but I know deep in my heart I still love him.

I don't have to wait long before Jamie and Graham arrive, their faces full of concern and touches of fear.

"Another one of our houses?" Jamie asks, her voice choked with emotion. "This can't be a coincidence. Someone is targeting us."

"There's another body?" Graham asks. He looks pale in the light of the streetlamp. "This house was vacant. It has to be another murder."

"Do they know who it is?" Jamie asks, clutching the collar of her jacket tight.

"Not yet. Ford did say the body had a gold tooth."

Graham's knees buckle and Jamie grabs him by the arm before he can fall. "You all right?"

"No," he says, struggling to stand. I lead him to a nearby car, and he leans against it. He lifts his glasses and rubs his eyes. "This can't be happening."

"What is it?" Jamie asks.

"I know who that is."

"Who?"

"Travis Cobb. The man dating my sister."

"How can you be so sure?" I ask.

"The tooth for one."

"Lots of people have a gold tooth. It's a style," Jamie says.

"But I just got in a fight with Travis last weekend and now he's here." He bends over, breathing heavily. "They'll think I did this."

"Nonsense. We know you didn't," I say, but I know Ford and Tyler will zero in on this new development. It doesn't look good.

"But you have an alibi for tonight," Jamie says with excitement.

"No, I don't. I was home in bed. No one will believe that."

"Say you were with me," Jamie says. "I'll back that up."

"You can't lie to the police," I jump in. "They'll find out and then you'll be in even more trouble."

"She's right. I appreciate your willingness to help me, but I can't let you lie," Graham says. "But I'm in trouble. Two people I know are dead and two of our houses are burned."

"The fight with you and Travis may have no bearing here," I say. "It might not even be him. What happened after your fight?"

"My sister, Evie, was so mad at me, she still hasn't talked to me."

"Did he file a police report?"

"No way. He's had plenty of his own trouble with the police. Drunk and disorderly, a DUI, a drug charge. Those are just the ones I know about. Travis was not a nice guy. Definitely not someone you want your sister dating. But Evie never listened to me."

"And now you have motive if that truly is Travis over there."

"I can find out," Graham says. "Let me call Evie. She'll know where he is."

Graham places the call and puts it on speaker. It goes directly to voicemail. He doesn't leave a message, just dials again.

This time, Evie answers. "I don't want to talk to you," she says.

"I know, but I need to talk to Travis. Do you know where he is?"

"Why?" Her voice is heavy with distrust.

"I just need to talk to him. Where is he?"

"If you must know, he was supposed to come here tonight, but he stood me up and isn't answering his phone. Thanks for rubbing it in."

"Evie, I think something happened to Travis," Graham says. "I think he may have been murdered."

"Stop being ridiculous. I don't appreciate this game."

"I'm not playing a game. I'm serious. One of our flip houses burned tonight and they found a body inside. It has a gold tooth."

"Lots of people have gold teeth," she says desperately.

"He's the only one I know, and I think someone is targeting me."

"Not everything is about you," Evie tries. "It has to be someone else. I'm calling Travis right now. I'm sure he's fine." The call ends.

The three of us stand in silence for a long moment. "Now what?" Jamie asks.

"I don't know. I'm sure Ford and Tyler will want to talk to you both seeing as this is your house." I twirl a length of my hair, thinking. "Graham, can you think of anyone that would want to frame you or hurt you?"

"Besides Travis, no."

"Nobody? I think you're right that you're being targeted in this horrible thing. There has to be someone that has it out for you."

"Dixie wasn't too happy with me when we broke up, but she's gone. Travis didn't like me beating him up, but he's gone too. I don't know anyone else that might hate me to this length. The only other thing in my life that might have any bearing on this is the tragedy with Maria. I've been over it from every angle I can, but I don't see how it's connected."

"What about Jason?" Jamie asks. "He was upset with you."

"That was nothing. We got it figured out."

"Jason, the roofer that commented on Dixie?"

"Yes. He and I had a dispute over some work he did. He thought I shorted him on the payment and it got pretty heated. We worked it out, though. I explained everything and we even shook hands on it."

"But he could be mad still," I say, knowing it's a stretch.

"Mad enough to kill two people I know and torch two houses?" Graham asks.

"Maybe," Jamie says, warming to the idea. "You didn't do it. I didn't do it. Who else is there?"

"How would he even know about Travis?"

"He was working on the roof the day you told me about the fight. He might have overheard. Plus, your knuckles were messed up a little. He could have noticed."

"Maybe," Graham says. "I can't picture it."

"Makes more sense than you," Jamie says.

"It's the only lead we have," I say. "I would imagine they already talked to Jason today, but I'm sure they will want to talk to him again now."

Graham takes off his glasses and rubs his eyes. "This is such a mess. Maybe I should leave town for a while."

"That's a bad idea," I say. "Will just make you look guilty. You have to stay and help with the investigation."

"What if they arrest me?" he asks in a strangled voice.

"They won't," I say with as much confidence as I can muster.

"You don't know that," he says.

"I know Ford and he will follow the law. They don't have any proof you did anything. It's just circumstantial."

"Circumstantial evidence is still evidence," he says miserably.

"Then all we can do is pray," I say.

TWENTY-THREE

JAMIE BLAKE

I want to grab Graham's hand and run. Drag him away somewhere safe. Ford, Tyler and the new detective I haven't met have their heads together and keep looking our way. It's scaring me.

I know in my heart that Graham wouldn't hurt anyone, let alone do these horrible things. I'd bet my life on it.

I lean next to Graham against a car, waiting. My hand reaches for his. Not to drag him away, but to offer what little comfort I can. His hand is rough and strong as he squeezes mine back.

The squeeze makes my belly tingle.

We've worked side by side for years, were friends before that. I know this man as well as I know myself, but we've never held hands like this. I know he's looked at me differently lately. A sentiment I've been too afraid to admit to myself.

It took a tragedy to make me see him for what he is.

The best man I know.

Rylan notices the hand-holding but doesn't comment on it. A tiny smile touches the corners of her mouth.

A smile that quickly disappears as Ford approaches with Tyler and the African American detective behind him.

"Thank you for waiting," he says formally. "You two must know this doesn't look good for you. This being the second house of yours where a victim has been found."

I shouldn't be surprised to be included in the comment. This is also my house. It still makes my blood run cold.

"We'll need you to come down to the station and make a formal statement," Tyler says, the other detective nodding along.

"I'm Detective Hudson," she says coldly. "I'll take the woman, you take him," she says to Tyler. She motions for me to follow her.

I let go of Graham's hand and feel untethered and loose. I don't like it.

"It's okay," Rylan says. "Just answer their questions and they will let you go soon."

I want to believe her as I go with Detective Hudson.

She gently helps me into the back of her car, thankfully without handcuffs. It's not until I'm in the uncomfortable backseat that it hits me. They think I'm a suspect, not just the owner of the burned house. Hence, the car.

Panic bubbles in my chest and I find it hard to breathe. Hudson climbs into the front seat and starts the car.

"Why are you taking me in? I could have just driven to the precinct like we did yesterday."

"The fact that we need to bring you in again should tell you all you need to know," she says cryptically. "You're not under arrest yet. Just tell us everything when we get there, and this will go more easily for you."

Her words don't quell the panic. I dig my fingernails into my palms and focus on the pain there to keep from losing it. "Everything will be okay," I tell myself. "Just keep calm."

Hard to do in the back of a cop car.

The ride seems to take forever, but we eventually reach the precinct and Hudson leads me into a small room with three chairs and a tiny table, the same room they questioned me in yesterday. I sink into one of the hard chairs.

Ford comes in and I realize right away that tonight the friendly air is gone. He's hard and all business, matching Hudson's tough ways. "I need to tell you this is being recorded and filmed," he says, getting right to it. "You are not yet being detained, only questioned. You are free to leave, but I recommend you answer our questions. Please state and spell your name."

I do as he says, then he dives into the meat of the matter.

"Do you know anyone with a gold tooth?"

I don't want to answer as I know it will look bad for Graham. I briefly think of lying, but the set of Ford's jaw tells me he will not believe me anyway. "I don't personally, but Graham thinks he knows the victim."

Ford's eyes widen the smallest fraction. "And who might that be?"

"Travis Cobb, his sister, Evie's, boyfriend."

Hudson writes this down. "How do you know that already? We just found the tooth tonight," she asks suspiciously.

"Rylan told us."

"Rylan, of course." She says this with more than a touch of sarcasm. "And Rylan knew how?"

I look to Ford for help. "I told her," he says.

Hudson doesn't look pleased at this. "Okay. So, Travis Cobb. Tell us about his relationship with Graham Rock."

I don't want to tell them about the fight between Graham and Travis. I take a deep breath and ask, "What do you want to know?"

"Anything you can tell us," Ford says.

"I don't know much," I stall.

"You're Graham's partner and must know him pretty well to

be holding his hand earlier," Hudson says. "I'm sure you know something about his relationship with his sister's boyfriend. Did he like him?"

I have no choice but to tell the truth. "No. He wasn't what you'd call a perfect boyfriend. I understand he has a record and wasn't nice to Evie."

"I see," Hudson says, writing down something.

"Did you know Travis?" Ford asks.

A surge of adrenaline courses through my blood at the question. "Not personally."

"But you knew of him," he pushes. "Knew he was openly cheating on Graham's sister."

"Graham mentioned it, yes. Then he told Rylan tonight."

"So you knew the victim. Did you know Dixie Campbell too?"

"Again, I knew of her, but I didn't know her personally."

"Did you know Graham was seen talking to her recently?" he pushes.

This shocks me. "No. Was he? He never mentioned it. I only know they used to date and broke up a few months ago."

"A witness saw a man who looks like him talking to Dixie not long before she was murdered."

I don't like the hard look of flint in his eyes or the way Hudson is staring at me expectantly.

"Graham did not do this," I say as firmly as I can.

"Okay, maybe not," Ford says.

"Did you?" Hudson asks.

The heightened adrenaline in my blood suddenly turns cold. "I did not."

They exchange a look. "You are pretty close to Graham. Could be you didn't like that he was talking to his ex," Hudson pushes.

"I didn't know," I say, my voice rising in fear.

"Both houses that were burned belonged to you. You knew they were vacant," she continues.

"I didn't do this," I plead. I look to Ford for backup, but he's a blank.

"Tell us what happened, Jamie," Ford says.

I don't know what to say or what to do. I feel like a fly caught in a web, nowhere to go.

Suddenly, I remember that they said I was free to go.

"I'm leaving."

"I wouldn't recommend that," Hudson says. "We need the truth."

"The truth is neither me nor Graham had anything to do with the murders. I don't know why the bodies were burned in our houses, except that someone is trying to frame us. Now, I'm out of here."

On wobbly legs, I stand and cross the tiny room to the door. "This is a mistake," Hudson says as I reach for the handle.

"You wasting time looking at us is the mistake. Go find the real killer." I turn the handle and sling the door open.

Out in the hall, Graham is leaving his interview room too. "Let's get out of here," he says and grabs me by the hand.

I know he means the precinct, but I wish he meant Ashby.

Out in the parking lot, we realize we don't have a car.

"Now what?" I ask miserably. It's the middle of the night, who could we call for a ride? I suppose the police would take us back to the scene, but I don't want to go in and ask. I just want to leave.

Graham is already on his phone.

"Who are you calling?" I ask.

"The only person I know is up right now, Rylan."

"Good thinking."

Rylan answers right away, and it turns out she was already headed our way. "I figured things might go down badly," she says on speakerphone. "I'll be right there."

I'm afraid the police are going to come out and arrest one or both of us. I keep checking the door behind us.

Graham must feel it, too, because he says, "Let's wait over there," and leads me to the end of the sidewalk, near some bushes.

It's only a few minutes until Rylan arrives. I let Graham sit in front and I climb into the huge backseat. Rylan doesn't ask any questions, although I'm sure she has plenty. I lean my head back on the headrest and close my eyes.

This morning feels like a world away and I am tired.

"I'm sorry you two are going through this," Rylan eventually says as she pulls up behind my car at the crime scene.

"I don't understand all of it," Graham says. I hate the hurt I hear in his voice.

"Is there anyone that might have it out for either of you? Anyone at all?" Rylan asks. "Maybe something from your past?"

"Nothing," I say.

"Seems death is following me," Graham says. "First Maria, then Dixie, now Travis."

TWENTY-FOUR

RYLAN FLYNN

The inside of my Cadillac is quiet after that statement.

Graham stares out the window at the remains of the burned house and the last fire truck just now leaving the scene. "This has to be about me. And now they're looking at Jamie too. I hate this."

"None of this is your fault. Not even Maria. There's something else going on here," I say. I debate telling them about Roland but decide against it. "We're just missing what it is," I add.

"I don't see any connections either. You sure it's not Maria's ghost? It's the only thing that makes sense. Even if it's only a little bit," Jamie says with pitiful hope.

"Or even Maria's parents," Graham adds.

"It's doubtful the Weinmans have come back into town just to murder two people you know and torch your houses," I say.

"So we're back to square one," Jamie says. "Or Maria."

"I just wish I knew where Maria's body went. They searched but didn't find her. That quarry was deep and had lots of crevices. I hate to think she just wasted away in one of them," Graham says.

"I could go see if I can talk to her," I say before I think about it.

"You'd do that?" he asks.

"Of course. It's possible her spirit is still here, waiting for her body to be found. I'd love to help her if I can or find out if she's behind these tragedies."

"When do you want to go?" he asks eagerly.

"How about in the morning? I don't want to go to an abandoned quarry in the dark. Besides, it's been a really long day and an even longer night," Jamie says.

She's right. It's very late and I'm very tired. "I can meet you there."

"You think you can really talk to Maria?" Graham asks.

"I'll do my best. If she's there and is willing to talk, I can."

He suddenly leans over and gives me a quick hug. "Thank you. Let's say at nine?"

"Nine it is," I reply.

He leans back so he can see Jamie in the backseat. "Ready to go? We should get some sleep."

"Am I going with you or is Rylan driving me home?"

His voice drops an octave and takes on a husky tone. "If you don't mind, I'd like you to come with me."

"Of course," she says, her own voice husky.

The car fills with a chemistry that makes me feel like an outsider. "Until tomorrow, then," I say.

Graham climbs out, then opens Jamie's door. In the rearview, I see him take her hand and lead her to his car.

Jamie has always said they were just friends. I doubt she'll say that after tonight.

Seeing Jamie and Graham finally together makes my separation from Ford feel all the more awful. I'd give anything to be falling into his bed tonight instead of returning to my house full of hoarded boxes and regrets. Anything except what he wants, my independence.

"You're being stubborn," I tell myself as I drive home. "He loves your independence, just not your recklessness."

Am I reckless? Sure, I've been in danger a lot lately, but was any of that avoidable? I suppose I could just stay home and watch TV with Mom and Elsa, but I don't see that happening. That's just not me.

If I'm to be honest, I thrive on chaos.

Can I change that?

Not while I'm seeing ghosts and chasing murderers.

I pull into my driveway and turn off the car. The headlights shine on the closed garage door and I stare at their glow.

Can I change?

Before I answer that, something slams onto the roof of my car. The accompanying howl confirms it's Roland. He jumps from the roof to the hood, the strings held tight over his head.

"I'm coming for you, Rylan," he hisses, then swings by the strings to the ground where he runs off into the night.

I sit in my car a long time after he is gone, not completely sure I saw him yet again.

I suddenly burst into tears of frustration and exhaustion, everything crashing in. I sit in the car until the sobs subside and I feel empty. I wipe at my eyes with the hem of my T-shirt and sniffle.

"Holy flip, get a grip," I grumble something I used to say back in middle school. The memory makes me smile.

Feeling better now, I let myself out of the car, hoping Roland doesn't reappear. I have to go around the house to the broken patio door to get in. Once inside, I hear the low murmur of the TV in Mom's room.

I glance inside and Elsa is on the bed with Onyx, watching an infomercial.

"Where's Mom?" I ask her.

"I don't know. She just disappeared a while ago."

"You should get some sleep and turn that off," I tell her.

"I'm a ghost. I don't have to go to bed," she says sweetly. "Besides, I like this one. The knives are so sharp, they cut everything."

I don't know how to respond to that, so I just say good night and head down the hall.

TWENTY-FIVE

FORD PIERCE

"Well, a good suspect just walked out the door," Faith Hudson says after Jamie leaves the interrogation room. "We just going to let her go?"

"That's all we can do," I say. "We don't have enough to book her and nothing to hold her on. Besides, I don't think she's the one. What's her motive?"

"She's mad at Graham for seeing Dixie behind her back."

"We both know that's weak. Besides, Rylan says they're just friends and business partners."

"Rylan again," Faith says sarcastically.

I bristle. "What's that supposed to mean? She's their friend."

"Just that it seems Rylan comes up at every turn in this investigation. Maybe she's the culprit. Ever think of that? She could be throwing heat on Graham to take it off herself."

I almost laugh out loud. "Rylan is not a killer."

"I'm just saying, she could be involved. You're just too close to see it."

I'm shocked at the junior detective's gumption. "What is that supposed to mean?"

"Everyone knows you two are dating. I call that conflict of interest." She says it politely, but it rankles just the same.

"For your information, we broke up. And I would never let my feelings for her get in the way of an investigation."

"I should hope not."

I'm breathing heavily and I force myself to calm down. It won't do for me to be at odds with this third member of the investigation team. Tyler opens the door before I can open my mouth and say something I'll regret.

"Graham left too," he says. "He admitted to knowing the victim as Travis Cobb and that he got in an altercation with him a while ago, but that's as far as I got. When I pushed, he just left. I didn't have anything to hold him on."

"We got the same out of Jamie," I tell him.

"Looks like we're at a dead end," Tyler says as we walk back to our office. "I checked on the roofer's alibi for Dixie's homicide, and it's solid. He was at a bowling alley, seen by many people. I confirmed with the manager. Seems it was league night and he knows Jason. I haven't asked about tonight yet, but it seems the two crimes must be related, so I doubt he's our guy."

"What about Dixie's coworker, Rebecca?" Faith asks as we enter the office. I sit at my desk and Tyler sits at his. Faith hangs out by the door. "She knew both victims and also Graham," she pushes.

"Let's go bring her in. It's the only lead we have at the moment," I say, grabbing my keys, nodding to Tyler and heading out of the office. Faith follows us down the hall. I suddenly realize it doesn't take all three of us to bring a woman in for questioning. "You stay here," I tell Faith and her face falls.

"Okay," she says, but I can tell she's not happy about it.

I feel like a jerk, but there's no way around it now. There's only room for two of us in the car anyway. Tyler drives to the address we have for Rebecca. I don't really think she's a good suspect, but the fact she went on a date with Travis Cobb the night before he was murdered means we need to at least talk to her.

I'm not really paying attention to the drive until we pull into my apartment complex. "Is this where Rebecca lives?" I ask.

"Yes. Just down this way," Tyler says. "Have you ever seen her around? She's kind of distinctive with that purple streak in her hair."

"No. I haven't." We park just around the corner from my building. "But I don't really know the neighbors."

The complex is quiet this late at night. I follow Tyler up the walkway to Rebecca's apartment. He knocks loudly on the door. I notice scratches on her door similar to the ones on mine. Before I can form a question about the scratches, the door opens a crack and Rebecca looks out.

Her face is soft and sleepy, her purple-streaked hair mussed. I sniff, wondering if she smells like smoke from the fire.

I only detect peppermint soap or shampoo. Not a trace of smoke.

"What's this all about?" she asks once she recognizes us. "I told you everything I knew back at Dixie's apartment." She doesn't sound pleased to see us.

"There's been a development," Tyler says.

"Travis Cobb has been murdered," I blurt to see her reaction.

She pales and steps back. "What do you mean?"

"His body was found at a fire earlier tonight," Tyler says. "We've come to ask when the last time you saw him was."

She continues backing up until she sinks into her couch covered with laundry. "I, don't. I mean, I saw him on our date, but not after that."

"I know this is hard," Tyler says. "But where were you earlier tonight?"

Her eyes grow wide with fear. "I was here. I've been here all night. I didn't go out or anything." Her voice fills with panic.

"Did anyone see you?" I ask.

"No. Wait, you think I did something to Travis? I barely know him."

"But you knew Dixie and you know Graham as well," I point out.

"I didn't hurt Dixie and I didn't hurt Travis. What does this have to do with Graham? I only met him a few times." Rebecca's voice turns high and thin.

"Travis was found in one of Graham's vacant houses as it burned down."

"Oh my," she gasps. "I didn't do that. I didn't do anything. I have no idea what happened to Dixie or to Travis now. Please, you have to believe me."

We're getting nowhere fast. I believe Rebecca, even though she seemed a viable suspect a few minutes ago. Still, I ask, "Can we look around a bit?"

She nods and sniffles. "Look all you want. I don't have anything to hide."

It only takes a few minutes to look over the small one-bedroom. I know the apartment well as it has the same layout as mine. I check the laundry room for clothes that might smell like smoke. I check for matches or lighters. I check the shower to see if it's been used recently or if the towels are dry.

I find nothing.

Tyler looks at me when I return and I shake my head.

"Look, I told you I didn't do anything wrong," Rebecca says, stronger now. "It is really late. I'd like it if you'd leave." She stands and opens the front door to let us out.

We don't have enough to bring her in or arrest her. We have no choice but to leave for now.

"We'll have more questions for you tomorrow," Tyler says.

"I will help any way I can," she says. "But you're wasting your time with me," she says as we walk out. As soon as we're on the sidewalk, she shuts the door.

"Well, that didn't go anywhere," Tyler says.

"I guess not," I agree.

We drive back to the office in tired silence. Faith is waiting for us and asks what happened. We tell her Rebecca was a dead end.

"Which leads us back to Graham and Jamie," Faith says.

"And nothing but circumstantial evidence to go on," I reply.

"Circumstantial could get us a warrant," she pushes back.

Tyler looks from me to her, noticing the tension. "What's up?"

"Faith thinks that Rylan is involved," I say simply. "I told her that isn't possible."

Tyler doesn't respond fast enough. "You too?" I ask.

"I didn't say that," he protests. "I was just wondering why she's been at both scenes in the middle of the night. Both times she was there before us. I don't think she would hurt anyone, but I do wonder why she was there."

"Last night, she saw the lights in the sky and was drawn to the scene to see if she could help. Tonight, she was invited by Aiden Andrews."

"The fire chief? What is he to Rylan?" Faith asks.

"I have no idea. I'm going to call Marrero and tell him we need a dental comparison on tonight's victim with Travis Cobb. Let's start there and get back on it in the morning."

I leave the interrogation room, planning on calling Marrero like I said. Instead, I just grab my jacket and head outside. I'll call on the way.

Right now, I need Rylan. Need to hear her voice. Need to smell her hair. Need to feel her skin.

I don't care what she's doing with Andrews. I don't care that she's mad at me.

. . .

Her house is dark when I pull in behind her Cadillac and turn off the car. I know this is foolhardy, but I don't care. Faith's accusations against her have me riled up.

I first go to the front door, planning on pounding on it until she opens. Then I remember all the stuff piled in front of the door. I make my way into the backyard and am startled by the broken glass on her patio.

She told me the puppet broke out of the house, I guess this is his handiwork. I slide the patio door open and let myself in before I think better of it.

"Rylan?" I call down the hall. I used to visit this house when I was growing up. Keaton's room is on the right. Rylan's is at the end on the left. I shimmy past the piles of boxes and head down the hall.

A TV plays in the master bedroom. Did she move into this room after her mom passed? I look in. An infomercial is playing, but no one is in there except the cat on the bed.

I close the door and turn toward Rylan's room.

She stands in the doorway, a dim light behind her.

"Who's there?" she demands.

"It's me."

"Ford?"

TWENTY-SIX

RYLAN FLYNN

The fear I felt when I heard someone in the house quickly morphs into anticipation.

Ford has come.

There's only one reason for him to be here. He needs to see me.

Then another option hits me.

"Is Keaton okay?" I ask. "Or Aunt Val?"

"Of course. That's not why I'm here." He takes a step closer.

"Why are you here?" I ask, barely able to breathe.

He takes another step. He's so close, I could touch him.

"I'm not sure. I just had to come." He's almost as breathless as I am.

"I thought you didn't want me anymore." I can't help the words swirling in my mind from slipping out.

"I've always wanted you. That's the problem. I can't stand it when you're in danger. But you have to be you. I can't change that."

"I could maybe be a bit more careful."

"Can you, though?" he asks honestly. "If this is to work, I need to accept you for who and what you are."

The words warm me, but now is not the time for words. I reach for the front of his shirt and pull him to me. His lips are hot and insistent, his hands find my body.

I lead him into my room and shut the door.

I am sure I'm dreaming when I wake up with Ford in my bed. He lies on his side, his back to me. I run a finger across his shoulders, enjoying the feel of his skin, reveling in his presence.

I could lie here all day, but the clock tells me I don't have much time until I need to meet Jamie and Graham at the quarry.

As if to wake me up, Onyx starts scratching at the door. The noise wakes Ford and he rolls to face me.

"Good morning," he says with a sleepy smile.

"Hey," I say, feeling nervous now that he's awake. "Did you sleep well?"

He reaches across my waist and pulls me against his chest. "Wonderfully," he murmurs into my hair. "You?"

"Good enough." I roll over so my back presses against his chest, the length of my body against him. "Too bad we have to get up."

"Do we?" he teases. "Let's just stay here." He begins running his hand down my thigh.

"We don't have time for that," I laugh, grabbing the hand that is making my skin tingle. "I need to go."

"Go where?" he says near my ear.

I suddenly don't want to tell him about another death connected to Graham, but I can't keep a secret from him. Not after the night we just shared.

"Do you remember Maria Weinman? She drowned at the quarry when we were in school."

"Oh yeah. I do remember that. She just disappeared in the water, right? I knew her brother a little bit. That was terrible."

"I'm going with Jamie and Graham to see if I can contact her ghost."

His hands stop roaming and he rolls onto his back. "That's sort of random. Why now and why with Jamie and Graham?"

"Graham was with her when she drowned. He told me about it last night. We don't really think it's related to what is happening now, but if Maria is stuck here, I'd like to help."

I brace for his reaction, sure he's going to be angry that I'm again involving myself.

"Always trying to help, aren't you?" Is that a touch of pride in his voice?

"Isn't that what you do? Didn't you become a cop so you could help people?" I shove up on my elbow so I can look him in the face. I feel like our whole relationship depends on how he handles this next sentence.

"We can both help in our way," he says, pushing a strand of hair away from my face. "If Maria Weinman needs you, then go to her."

The tension leaves my body, and I lower my head to his chest and snuggle against him.

"Thank you," I whisper so low I don't think he can hear it.

Onyx scratches at the door and lets out a loud meow. "Looks like the alarm is going off," Ford says with a chuckle. "I need to get back to work too." He kisses the top of my head and then we both sit up.

"Any headway on the cases?" I ask as we get dressed.

"Not really. I expect to have verified the victims' identities this morning. Marrero was going to run dental comparisons. Once we have the confirmed identities, we can go forward."

"Sorry I kept you up late," I tease.

"I'm not." He grins mischievously. "Don't regret a thing."

I grab my jacket and follow him into the hall.

"Oh yeah," he says. "Last night, the TV was on in your mom's old room." He stops by the door. "It's off now."

"I, um, I was watching in there and I must have left it on. I think it has a timer." I hope he'll buy the story. "Ready to go?"

We go out to the kitchen. He looks at the broken patio door. "You should put something over that hole. I'm surprised the cat hasn't gone out or something hasn't come in."

"Yeah, I need to do that. I'll try to get to it today. I'm sure I can find something in all this mess that will work."

He looks around the piles. "I noticed your room was clear. That's good. Do you have plans for the rest of the house?" There's no hint of condemnation, just curiosity.

"If I can find the time, I think I'm ready to start getting rid of things. To be honest, I don't understand how it got this way."

"It happens," he says carefully.

"I should have done better. Mom trusted me with her house, and I don't think she's very happy with what I've done to it." Too late, I realize how this statement sounds.

Luckily, Ford doesn't notice. "I'm sure she's watching from heaven and just worries about you. She'd never judge you."

"I judge myself."

"Tell you what. When this case is wrapped up, I'll come help you clear some of it out. Just what you're comfortable with getting rid of. No pressure."

I look at the piles of things I once treasured and carefully collected. There's so much of it, I feel overwhelmed. Can I get rid of things? The stuff has kept me safe. At least that's how I felt about it.

The danger was in Keaton's room all along and the boxes didn't keep it there.

"I think I can do that. It would be nice to have some space in here."

"Great. We'll look into it when we have the time. For now, we need to go."

I check the time and he's right. I'm going to be late even

leaving now. I take the time to give him a good kiss, then slide what's left of the patio door open.

"We need to at least clear a path to the front door," he says.

I wholeheartedly agree with that. "I often wonder if the neighbors see me always using the back door and what they think," I say as we approach the cars.

"You won't have long to worry about it." He pulls me close. "Let's give them something else to watch." His lips press mine right there in the driveway in the bright morning sun.

I could start my day like this all the time.

TWENTY-SEVEN

RYLAN FLYNN

Jamie and Graham lean against the hood of their car, waiting for me at the gate to the quarry. They stand very close together. Something's obviously changed in their relationship, and it makes me smile.

A large NO TRESPASSING sign is on the metal gate. The bright orange letters give me pause. This isn't exactly legal.

I look down the dirt road. No one's around.

"We really going to do this?" Jamie asks when I join them. She motions to the sign. "Won't we get in trouble?"

"We're already in trouble," Graham says. "Besides, that sign has been there forever. This place was abandoned long before we came here in high school. No one cares."

"Let's go," I say and begin climbing the gate. I get to the top and look down. Jamie is still standing by her car, but Graham is right beside me.

"You coming?" I ask her.

"I don't feel right about this."

"Why are you stalling?" Graham calls down. "Don't you want to do this?"

"I just—"

Jamie can hear ghosts, even if she can't see them. I suddenly realize she's scared.

"There's nothing to be afraid of. I'll be right there, and Maria, if she is here, won't hurt you. She's just a kid."

"That's what you keep saying, but we don't really know, do we? She may have killed two people."

"Even more reason for us to go see her if she's here," Graham says. "To clear our names."

"I know that." Jamie rubs her hands together. "I'm just not used to doing this like you are," she says to me. "Each time terrifies me."

"Come on, babe. We can do this. I'm scared too." Graham throws his leg over the gate and starts down the other side.

"Fine. I'm coming." Jamie starts climbing.

Soon we're all walking the gravel drive toward the flooded quarry. The sun shines and the birds sing in the trees that push in on the lane. It's almost a lovely morning. If we weren't going to see a dead girl.

We walk in somber silence, each lost in thought. Soon, the trees give way and the expanse of water stretches before us.

The lane turns to the right and leads to an abandoned building with a vehicle scale. A few sheds sit behind the building. The entire property is full of weeds and has an air of decay.

"This way," Graham says, leading us to the left. "This is where we used to jump off. There's a path up from the water, right there. It's all grown over now."

I step to the edge of a high wall and look over. Somehow, I pictured the cliff as taller than it is. The dark water lies maybe twelve feet down.

"Seemed so much scarier back then," Graham says, peering over the edge with me.

"Do you sense anything?" Jamie asks, avoiding the edge but glancing around.

I take mental stock of my body, hoping to feel a tingle in my back.

"Not really," I say, disappointed. "Do you hear anything?"

Jamie shakes her head. "Nothing but the birds and the wind."

"She has to be here," Graham says, almost desperate. "I need to talk to her again."

"Let me try something." I face the water and open my arms wide, palms up. "Lord, let us see Maria. Let us talk to her. If she is here, she may need us. Please, Lord."

The wind shifts and picks up. The tingle in my back starts low in my spine.

"Lord, please bring her to us. Let us learn the truth and lead her soul to You."

The dirt swirls up and before me stands a young woman. Her long dark hair is wet and sticks to her face. She's dressed in a blue bikini.

"Maria?" I ask, dropping my hands back to my sides.

Her head whips my way so fast, her hair flies out.

"You can see me?" she asks.

Jamie gasps. "I heard something."

"I can see you. My name is Rylan. Are you Maria Weinman?"

"I am." She looks shyly from me to Jamie, then her eyes land on Graham. "Why does he look familiar?"

"That is Graham Rock," I tell her.

"He's too old to be Graham," Maria says.

"It's been a long time since you've seen him."

Maria walks around him, studies his face. "Has it been that long? I can't keep track here."

"Maria, we're here to help you. I wasn't even sure you'd still be here, but I wanted to try."

"Why help me? I don't know you."

"I'm a friend of Graham's. He told me what happened."

"Who's this?" Maria asks about Jamie.

"I'm Jamie. A friend."

Maria's eyes widen. "She can see me too?"

"I can only hear you," Jamie replies. "I can't see you. I'm so sorry about what happened to you."

Maria shrugs. "I was terribly sad at first. I watched them search for my body, but they never found it, no matter how many times I explained to them where it is."

"Can you tell me?" I ask.

"It's over there," she points across the water toward a tree. "I'm not sure how it got there, but I've seen it lots of times. Not much left now. Just bones."

"Do you know how you died?" I ask.

Graham seems very interested in this question.

"Graham and I decided to jump in the water. We went in holding hands. I hit the water wrong, I think. I know it's not too far down, but somehow it knocked all the air out of me and I let go of his hand. I tried not to breathe in before I came up, but I did. Then I think a current got a hold of me, because I ended up on that ledge."

I tell Graham what she said. He almost collapses with the information.

"I've thought all this time it was my fault. It was just an accident."

"Oh, it wasn't your fault," Maria says. "I've had a long time to think about it and the only conclusion I can come to is that it was just my time."

I tell Graham what she said.

"Thank you," he tells me somberly.

"Maria, have you been here at the quarry all this time? Have you gone anywhere else?" I ask the leading question.

Her face is open and her eyes clear when she says, "I've never left here."

"Not even to go to Ashby?" I push.

"No. Why would I?"

"Some things have been happening in Ashby, and we wondered if you knew about them," Jamie says.

"What sort of things?" she asks.

"There have been two murders and two of Graham and Jamie's houses have been burned."

"Murder?" she asks breathlessly. "Why would I know about that?"

"We just thought," Jamie says, then stops. "I don't know what we thought." She looks to me for help.

"We've been trying to find out who might have a reason to want to frame Graham. The murders and the arsons are all tied to him."

Maria takes a step away from me. "I wouldn't do that. I couldn't do that. I'm already dead, in case you forgot. I couldn't murder anyone."

"It was a long shot, but we had to ask," I try, lifting my hands.

"You call it a long shot, I call it a horrible accusation. Just get away. I don't want to see you even if you can see me." She crosses her arms and puts on a pout, but I notice she's watching Graham for his reaction.

"We will leave if that's what you want," I say, starting down the path and pulling Graham with me.

"Wait," she says. "Wait. I'm so lonely here. No one ever comes. I don't understand why I'm still here all alone."

"We have to help her. She deserves some peace," Jamie says.

"Do you mean cross to heaven?" she asks hopefully.

"I can help you cross when the time is right. I think we need to find your remains first. I'm sure your family would like to have some small part of you back." I feel morbid talking like this.

"Especially my brother," Maria says. "He seems to have taken my death the hardest."

I don't have the heart to tell her one brother is in prison and the other is dead.

With promises to return soon, we leave Maria at the quarry and make our way back to the gate. I tell Graham every detail of the conversation on the way.

"You don't think she's behind the murders?" he asks.

"I really don't. It was a long shot."

"What happens now?" Graham asks.

"Now we need to bring the authorities in so they can find her remains and return them to her family. Then I'll try to cross her over. Beyond that, I don't know."

"Who can we call?" Jamie asks. "Ford thinks we're murder suspects and he's busy with the investigation. I doubt he'll want to take the time to find a missing girl from over a decade ago."

"Maybe not Ford," I agree. "But I know someone else that might be interested. Besides, Maria's death was ruled an accident, I don't think that falls under police jurisdiction anymore. It would fall to the fire department."

"And the fire chief," Jamie says. "We saw how he looked at you. I'm sure he'll do anything you ask."

"I don't know about that," I hedge. I want to tell them I'm back with Ford, but he's not exactly their favorite person right now. I don't know how they'd take it.

"You'll call him?" Graham pushes.

"I'll call."

I don't have Aiden's direct number, so I have to call the fire department and hope for the best. It doesn't take too long until he's on the line.

"Rylan? To what do I owe this honor?" he asks with good humor.

"Uh, I need your help."

"Okay. What kind of help?"

I explain about Maria's remains and how they need to be found.

"I'm not exactly sure that's something we can do," he says.

"Why not? Don't you have a dive team for things like this?"

"Well, yes, but I think this is a police matter. Once the police ask us, we can come and find her."

"But it's already ruled an accident, doesn't that take it away from the police?"

"I don't know for sure. This is the first time a ghost has told us where to find her body." He sounds like he's enjoying this.

"It's not funny to Maria," I say.

"I know. I know. Look, why don't you run this by Pierce or Spencer and let them get the ball rolling. Then I'd be happy to send our team out to find her."

I suppose that's the best I can hope for. Especially considering that the information comes from a ghost. I can't imagine Aiden wants to tell his team he's following orders from a dead girl.

I hang up the phone and ponder what to do next. I hate to ask for a favor so close to making up with Ford. I wish I was a diver; I'd just go find her myself.

But Maria deserves to be treated with respect. She needs the professionals.

Taking a deep breath, I place the call to Ford.

"Pierce," he answers. This throws me a bit.

"Uh, hi. It's Rylan," I say.

"Sorry, Ry. I didn't look at who was calling. Things are nuts around here right now. We got the identification back on last night's body. It's Travis. Busy lining up talks with his family and friends. You know the drill."

"I hate to bother you, but I wanted your advice on something."

"You're no bother at all. What's up?"

"Let's say a ghost tells me where her body is. She died by

accident but needs to be found. Who would be in charge of that?"

"You talked to Maria Weinman? She's still there?"

"Yes. She's been waiting for someone to find her, I think. Can you help?"

He takes a long time to answer. "I don't know what to tell Chief McKay about a ghost telling you where she is."

"That's basically the same thing Aiden said."

Too late, I realize I shouldn't have mentioned Aiden.

"You called him already?" Ford asks tightly.

"Just now. I didn't think it would be a police matter, so I called the fire department."

A long beat of silence.

"I'll see what I can do." His voice is still tight. He has a right to be mad. I should have called him first. "Look, I need to go."

"Okay. Thank you." I want to say more, but I don't know what that would be. It doesn't matter. He's already ended the call.

TWENTY-EIGHT

The burning of the house doesn't quench the fire in my chest. I think of the moment the man died at my hand, his gold tooth glinting as I strangled him. That doesn't help either.

The vision changes to his face. The man I seek to destroy.

Death is too easy for him.

I need him to pay.

I need to take away everything valuable to him.

A different face comes to mind.

This time I smile.

The puppet next to me smiles too. "She's perfect," he hisses. "Take her and make him pay."

TWENTY-NINE

RYLAN FLYNN

I have a lot on my mind, but no direction to work in. I think about going to Aunt Val's donut shop, but it's her day off and that's across town. I drive around a little while, listening to Red Hot Chili Peppers turned way up, hoping the music will give me some direction. It doesn't and I eventually find myself back at home.

I let myself in through the broken patio door, then look for something to patch it with. After a lot of searching, I find a piece of cardboard and some duct tape. Soon, the hole is covered.

I turn around to find Mom watching me tape the door.

"You're home," she says warmly.

I place the last piece of tape. "You weren't here last night," I counter. "I've always wanted to know where you all go." I pull open the junk drawer in the kitchen and put the tape away.

Mom just shrugs. "I had something I wanted to check on."

"It worked out, because Ford came over."

Mom clutches her hands together. "I'm so happy for you. So you all made up?"

"Yes. But now I think he's annoyed with me again." I tell her about Maria and how I called Aiden first. "I really just wanted what was best for Maria. I didn't have any ulterior motive in calling him."

"I'm sure it will be okay. You both have a lot going on with the murder of that girl."

"There's been another murder." I explain about Travis and Graham and Jamie being questioned.

"Oh my. You've been busy."

"I have. I wanted to ask you about a ghost I met last night at the courthouse. Her name is Jean, her maiden name was Flynn. Do you know anything about her? She was killed back in the 1920s. Her husband pushed her off the balcony at the courthouse and she broke her neck. He passed it off as a suicide."

"I seem to remember your grandma mentioning suicide in the family once, but I don't know the details. You met this Jean?"

"Last night. Stan the security guard thought there might be a spirit there and last night she started breaking things. Mickey and I went. Oh yeah, get this. Did you know that Lindy Parker and I are distant cousins or something?"

"Lindy? Oh my, I'm sorry," she says with a half-smile.

"Jean's sister is her great-great-grandma and her brother is who Dad is named after."

"Well, it's a small town. If you go back far enough, nearly everyone is related."

"I get that, but Lindy?"

"She can't be that bad. You two are both grown now."

"Trust me. She still hates me as much as she did back in school," I say.

"Just keep avoiding her and focus on what you need to do."

"I have plenty to do. Holy flip, I almost forgot to tell you. The puppet showed up at the courthouse and we think the spirit inside him is Jean's husband. The one that killed her."

"How is that possible?"

"The same way Elsa was in Darby. His name is Roland and he owned the puppet way back then. Was a gift."

"That's interesting. At least you know what you're dealing with now."

"Do I?"

"More than you did before. When are you going back to see Jean?"

"I was hoping tonight. She wants to see her family, though. I think Dad and Val would come, but I was sort of hoping Keaton would too."

"That's ambitious," Mom says, not unkindly.

"Whatever it takes to cross her. She wants family. I'll bring her who I can."

"You know what you're doing."

"Do I?" I ask honestly. "I feel like I'm just running in circles lately. So many crimes in this town, I can hardly keep up."

"What are you saying?"

"I think something dark is in play around here. And I should be getting to the bottom of it. It all starts with the puppet. I wish I knew where it was right now. It jumped on my car last night but ran away. I'm pretty sure it's attached to me somehow."

Mom thinks this over. "Why would Jean's husband be attached to you? That's not good. What are you going to do about it?"

"I have no idea." The cat suddenly leaps up on a pile of stuff behind Mom. Half the pile tumbles and Onyx jumps away to safety, but my heart pounds in reaction.

"You know, I haven't wanted to say anything, but you really need to clean up this house," Mom says.

"I know. It kind of got out of hand. I'm sorry."

"You don't need to be sorry, but this can't be healthy for you."

"Ford said it's a grief response."

"It probably is, but you still need to make progress. Maybe start with just a few things. When does the trash pick up?"

I try to remember what day it is. "I think in the morning."

"Perfect. Let's clear out a little space here in the dining room and throw it out."

Panic shudders through me. "You mean, throw it in the trash?"

"You'll feel better with less stuff."

"I can help," Elsa pipes in, suddenly appearing. I wonder if she's been listening the whole time from the hall. "I like to move boxes."

The thought makes my palms sweat, but I know it needs to be done. "Maybe this stack. It's dangerous." I pick up a frying pan I've never used that has fallen to the floor. "I can do this," I say and toss it in the trash. "But let's start with the front door. Then I can use it."

"That's my girl. Now let's get to work."

The three of us spend the rest of the morning clearing out a walkway to the front door. It was hard to get started, but soon I'm in the groove. Each item and box I throw out makes my soul feel lighter. Elsa even throws a few boxes in the roll-away bin. Mom manages to pick up a stray sock.

Finally, there's space to open the door. I turn the knob and pull the door open. "Now I won't have to go around back every time I want to leave."

Mom and Elsa stand together, beaming with pride. "It's a start," Mom says. "I'm proud of you."

"I can keep cleaning when you're not here," Elsa says. "I like moving things. Reminds me of when I was alive."

This statement leaves Mom and I standing silent. I've been so busy since Elsa came, I haven't given much thought to how she feels about being here on this side. I should cross her. I know I should.

But Elsa has a reason for still being here. I thought it was to tell her parents she was okay, but they won't listen to me at all.

I do know of a stuck spirit that I can help today. I call Dad and Val and even Keaton about Jean. Dad and Val agree to help immediately. Keaton reluctantly agreed. We plan to meet at midnight at the courthouse. I even call Stan to make sure we'll be able to get in.

Everything is set for Jean.

If only I could help Maria today too.

I don't want to annoy Ford with my request, but as the afternoon moves on, I can't help but wonder if he talked to Chief McKay or even Aiden to see if we can recover Maria's remains.

I keep pulling my phone out of my pocket and checking it.

"Just call him," Mom finally says. "See what's up."

Mom's right. I'm being silly. If he's busy, he won't answer. I have nothing to lose by calling him.

I place the call and Mom and Elsa watch me expectantly as I wait for him to answer.

"Hey, Ry. I was just getting ready to call you," Ford says.

"Oh really? About what?"

"Chief McKay agreed to a search for Maria Weinman's remains. He talked to the fire department and they're sending out a team today. Looks like you have some believers on your side."

"Thank you for asking. I truly appreciate it."

"You should have asked me first," he says.

"I know. I wasn't thinking. I didn't know what to do."

A long moment of silence, then he continues in a much better mood, "I'll be there if that's okay? I'd like to see her brought home."

"I'd love that. What time?"

"In an hour. Does that work?"

THIRTY

RYLAN FLYNN

This time I don't have to climb the gate to get to the quarry. The chain is off and the gate hangs open. The place is much more active now than it was this morning. A fire truck and Aiden's official truck are already here. Two police cruisers are also here as well as Ford's black Malibu parked next to the abandoned building.

I park behind Ford's car and get out. He's talking to a uniformed officer that I don't recognize, but crosses the gravel lot when he sees me.

"The divers just got here," he says. "They're setting up now."

Here by the building, the divers can just walk into the water, not jump from the overhang. A man and a woman in wetsuits are donning tanks and masks.

"All we need now is to know exactly where to look," Ford says.

"Maria said she was over there on an underwater ledge."

"Can she be more specific? Is she here now so you can talk to her?" he asks.

I look around the clearing and up the path to where people jump off. "I don't see her."

"Can you call out to her?"

"I can try."

I feel self-conscious with the fire department and police officers here, but I close my eyes and focus.

"Maria, are you here?" I call.

Nothing happens. No tingle, no Maria. When I open my eyes, everyone is watching me, even the divers. It seems everyone knows who I am and why I'm here.

"Maybe I'll have better luck up on the cliffs where we saw her before," I say as much to escape the scrutiny as because I think it will help.

"I'll come with you," Ford says and follows me up the path.

Once on top, I look down at the water. It makes my stomach churn, so I step away from the edge.

"Let's try this again," I say and close my eyes, my arms out and palms open to the sky.

"Maria, we need you. I have everyone here to find your remains. I just need you to show me where they are."

A tingle creeps up my spine and I open my eyes.

"I didn't think you'd come back," Maria says, her hair dripping. "When I saw all the people, I got scared."

"You don't have to be scared. They're all here for you."

She looks pointedly at Ford. "Who's this?"

"This is Ford. He's a detective. He put this search party together for us."

"You're really going to find my body? There isn't much left other than bones." She sniffles softly, prettily. "Now I can cross to heaven."

"I would think so. First things first. I need to tell the divers where to look."

"There's a ledge just below that tree on the far side about fifty feet underwater. They will find me there."

I tell Ford and he starts down the trail to tell the divers.

Maria watches him go. "What happens now?"

"Now the divers will go look for you and bring you back up. I don't know after that."

"Will you stay with me while they do this?" she asks, sounding like the young girl she is.

I nod. I wish I could take her hand, but settle for standing near her. We watch in companionable silence as the divers swim toward the tree with a large bag. They then go under, their bubbles leaving a trail above them.

"It's nice there, right?" Maria asks. "Heaven, I mean."

"I don't know, but I imagine it is," I say gently.

Several silent minutes later, the divers surface with the bag. One of them gives a thumbs up across the water to the others standing on the bank.

"They have you," I say.

Maria turns to face me, her face wet with tears. "Thank you," she says, her voice choked. "I thought no one would ever come."

"You should thank Graham. He's the one that told me about you."

"I thought I loved that boy once," she says. "He's all grown up now. A man really. It's strange. I still feel fourteen, but also so much older." She wipes the tears from her cheeks. "I think I'm ready to go."

I expected a light to open when they found the bones, but there's not even a glimmer.

"So, how does this work? Is there a light like they say?"

"Yes, normally there is. I don't understand why there isn't one now."

Maria looks worried. "No light? Does that mean I'm stuck here?"

"Let me try something." I turn my face to the sky and begin praying out loud for God to take her.

"I don't think it's working," Maria says, worried.

I repeat the simple prayer, but I know it's pointless. "I don't think now is your time," I say somberly.

"Why not?"

"I don't know."

"So I'm stuck?"

"I'm sorry," I say. "I really thought I could help you cross today. But only God decides the time."

"So I have to stay here all alone? Like, forever?" She pushes wet hair behind her ear.

"I doubt it. Maybe there's some reason you're still here."

"But I don't want to be here. I want to cross over. My grandma died the year before I drowned. I bet she's in heaven just waiting for me."

"She might be. I don't know what else I can do for you right now."

Maria shoves both her hands into her long hair in frustration. "But I don't want to stay here."

"I don't know for sure, but I think you can go to other places. I know a spirit that travels where she wants," I say, thinking of Elsa and how she travels.

Maria looks up at me with hope. "I can leave the quarry?"

"Maybe. You could try it. Is there anywhere you would like to go?"

"I want to see my family. How does this work? Do I walk to their house?"

"I think you just focus on where you want to go and you appear there."

Maria scrunches her face in concentration. For a long moment, nothing happens.

Then she disappears.

"Looks like you were right," Ford says when I rejoin the activity by the abandoned building. "They found her bones on a ledge just where you said."

Sideways glances and outright stares come from the fire-fighters and officers at the scene. Some of them look afraid of me, some look impressed.

"I just told you what Maria said."

"Did she cross over?"

"No. But she went to visit her family. At least she was trying to."

"Still here then?"

I don't get the chance to answer. Aiden Andrews approaches, hand outstretched for me to shake. "Well done, Rylan. You have amazed me again. This ghost talk stuff must be real. I mean, I already believed you, but this, this is really cool."

I shake his hand, but feel silly about it. "Maria just told me where she was."

"But you talked to her."

"That's what Rylan does," Ford says, inching closer to me.

Aiden looks from him to me, then nods. "I see. Well, I'm still impressed and I'm glad we can bring the family some closure."

"Me too," I say, then touch Ford's shoulder to drive the point home that I'm not interested in Aiden beyond professionally.

Aiden nods again and walks away.

"You know that guy has a thing for you," Ford says.

"But I only have a thing for you," I say and give his hand a quick reassuring squeeze.

Gravel crunches and the coroner's van pulls up next to us. Marrero is driving and glares through the windshield at us. Did he see me hold Ford's hand?

"I should go," I say.

Marrero jumps from the van and stares me down before I can escape. "I hear you found another body. This one underwater," he says.

"I didn't find it exactly. I just repeated what the ghost told me," I say, lifting my chin.

"I will never understand how you do it, but one of these days, I will prove you're making up the ghost thing."

"I'm not making it up."

"She's not making it up," Ford says at the same time.

Marrero looks from me to Ford then back to me. "We'll see." He stalks away toward the bag of bones.

"Man, that guy doesn't like you," Ford says. "What did you ever do to him?"

"I have no idea. I think he feels threatened somehow. I've been treated worse."

"You'd think he'd appreciate what you do."

"Maybe someday. Look, I'm going to get out of here before he gets more angry. I have to cross a ghost at the courthouse tonight. I'd like a little rest before that."

"The courthouse? I didn't know it was haunted."

"By a distant relative, no less. She wants to see the family before she crosses."

"Oh, I bet Keaton just loves that."

"He's agreed to come tonight."

"That's a surprise," he says, raising his eyebrows.

"He wasn't too happy about it, but I explained it was the only way to get Jean to go."

Ford shakes his head with a little smile on his lips. "Good luck. Do you want some company afterward? I'm sure I'll have to work late, but I can come over when I'm done."

"I'd love that. Oh, yeah, you can use the front door now."

"You cleaned?"

"Yep," I say as I get in my car. "You inspired me."

THIRTY-ONE
RYLAN FLYNN

"Do you want me to come with you?" Mom asks as I get ready to go to the courthouse and Jean.

"I can come too," Elsa chimes in. "It might be fun."

"No. You both should stay here."

"But I could see Keaton," Mom pushes.

I don't have the heart to remind her Keaton wouldn't even know she was there.

"We went to the courthouse on a field trip once. It was so pretty. Please, can we come?" Elsa says. "I promise I'll be good."

"I know you'd be good, but Jean will be able to see you and I don't want—" I stop mid-sentence.

"You don't want to tell anyone about us?" Mom finishes for me.

I feel ashamed. "I haven't told about you. I-I just wanted to keep you for myself. No one else can see you anyway."

"That's okay," Mom says gently.

"But your friends already know about me," Elsa says. "They were there when you burned the bear I was stuck inside. Can I come?"

"I need to focus on Jean tonight. I'm sorry," I say as I tie my sneakers.

Elsa crosses her arms and huffs. "You can't stop me," she grumbles. "I don't get to do anything."

"We can do something tomorrow. Please, just stay here tonight." I pull my hair back into a ponytail and I'm ready. "Right now, I need to go."

"You're always going somewhere," Elsa pouts.

"Elsa, Rylan has an important job to do. We can't bother her now," Mom says.

"I'll tell you all about it when I get back. Have a good night." I hurry to the front door, admiring the open space but taking mental note that there's a lot of work to do still to clear the house.

The courthouse is beautiful in the night. Mickey is waiting on the front steps for me, camera in hand. She gives me a hello and a quick hug as Keaton parks.

"This takes the cake," he says. "You bring us all out at midnight on a wild ghost chase?" he says, striding up the sidewalk. Behind him, Aunt Val parks and Dad pulls in beside her.

"This isn't a wild ghost chase. Jean wanted us all here. She wants to see her family before she passes," I explain again.

"Her distant family. So her brother is our great-grandpa or something. That was a long time ago."

"To some people, family is important. Besides, Dad said he remembered Brett. At least a little bit," I say as Dad and Aunt Val join us. Dad has his Bible in his hands.

"That's right," Dad says. "I was just a kid, but I knew I was named after him, so I thought he was a superhero or something."

"I don't remember him at all," Aunt Val adds. "I wish I did."

"You were pretty young when he died," Dad consoles.

I change the subject. "Looks like we're all here. Ready for this?"

Everyone seems prepared, but Keaton has a strange look on his face. To Mickey, this is common, and Dad has crossed many spirits with me. Even Aunt Val has done this. For Keaton, watching me work is all new.

"Don't worry," I say, clapping him on the back. "She won't hurt you. You just have to be here."

"I'm not worried. This is just a little nuts."

I don't like that word, but let it slide. "Let's go in. Stan should be waiting for us."

Stan is behind the glass doors and opens them for us, then leads us to the lobby. "Where do you want to do this?" he asks.

"I think here where she landed and died should be good," I say. "Have you heard her tonight?"

"I haven't. You think she'll show?"

"I hope so. This is what she wanted," I say, noticing the tingle beginning at the base of my spine. "I think she's here now."

Mickey turns on the camera and everyone else waits expectantly.

"Where is she?" Val whispers.

Jean materializes on the steps, making quite an entrance, even if it's only for my benefit. "So, you came after all?" she says.

"She's here. On the steps," I tell the camera.

Keaton shifts in his expensive shoes. "She's really here?"

Jean's head swivels at this. "Doesn't he believe in me?" she asks.

"This is my brother, Keaton. This is his first time meeting a ghost."

"Oh, I know this one. I see him here all the time. I even saw him kissing his receptionist in the storage room," she says.

"That's his fiancée," I explain.

Jean shrugs and crosses to the center of the lobby. "No matter. Can't choose your family, can you?" She moves close to Dad and Val, studying them. "This is Brett's namesake?"

"Yes. This is my dad, Brett Flynn. He was just saying he remembers your brother a little bit."

"You don't say? Tell me, did Brett keep his hair? He was always so vain about it."

I try not to laugh as I ask Dad what he remembers of his great-grandpa's hair.

"As I recall, it was gray but thick," Dad says.

"Figures," Jean says. "Brett always got what he wanted." She turns her attention to Val. "This one looks like my mamma."

"Jean says you look like her mamma," I tell Val.

"I'm glad," Val murmurs.

"Okay, now where is the other one so we can get this show on the road?" Jean asks.

"What other one?" I ask.

"That distant cousin of yours. My sister's granddaughter. The one that I threw the book at."

"You mean Lindy? Why do we need her?" I ask, panic rising.

"She's family too. I want her here when I cross."

"Lindy will never agree to come. Plus, she has many cousins and stuff that are also related. We'd have to have half the town here if we start that."

Jean thinks for a moment, and I worry she will want me to invite them all. "I suppose you all will have to do. At least I know the Flynn bloodline is strong and carrying on without me."

"So you're ready?" I ask.

"I'm tired of waiting around here. You all know now that I didn't hurt myself. It's too late for justice or to say goodbye to anyone I knew."

"Before you go, what can you tell me about the puppet and Roland?" I ask, leading Jean to the far side of the lobby, away from everyone.

Jean waves a hand. "Oh that nasty thing? Imagine Roland stuck in that puppet I hated." She laughs. "I suppose maybe it wasn't too late for justice after all."

"Are you sure it's Roland in the thing? I feel like it's an evil spirit in there."

"Well, Roland was evil, at least to me." She rubs her neck. "He killed me after all. Then told everyone I did it to myself. What my poor mother must have gone through. I hate to think of it."

"The puppet with Roland in it is influencing bad things in town. What can I do to stop him?" I ask, a bit breathless.

Jean shrugs one shoulder, her red dress slipping a little. "How should I know? You're the ghost hunter. Go hunt him."

I don't like this answer, but I'm not going to get anything out of Jean on the subject.

"Can we get this show on the road, please?" she says.

"What's going on?" Keaton calls. "We don't want to be here all night."

"Jean is ready," I say, crossing the lobby back to my family and the camera. "I wish you lots of luck," I say to Jean.

"Here's hoping the other side is better than this one," Jean says. "Now do it."

"I can't promise this will work." I'm thinking of Maria and how I wasn't able to help her.

"Just try."

I look to Dad, and he opens the Bible and begins to read from Psalms.

"Everyone bow your heads and pray for Jean's soul," I say. Stan and Val drop their heads instantly, Keaton looks at me incredulously.

"Just go along," I tell him.

He drops his head, but I doubt his eyes are closed.

Dad continues reading and Jean waits expectantly. I hear a nervous giggle down a hall. I turn to look and see Elsa and Mom hiding in the shadows.

"Who's there?" Jean demands, turning.

I don't know what to do. They should not have come.

I try to wave them off without anyone seeing, but they don't get the hint. I give up. I can't even glare at them with the camera filming me.

Ignoring them, I turn back to Jean. "Focus on me," I tell her, and she looks away from Mom and Elsa. "This is your time."

Jean looks annoyed at the intrusion but returns her attention to me. Dad is still reading, and I recite along with the words.

Soon, a familiar light opens in the lobby.

"I see it!" Jean cries out.

"The light is here," I say for the benefit of the camera. "It's working."

Jean walks to the light, her face rapt with excitement. "Mama, I'm coming."

She steps through the doorway and as quickly as it opened, it closes.

"It's over," I tell everyone. "She's crossed."

"Way to go, Rylan!" Elsa shouts as they come out of the hallway and join us.

I ignore them the best I can as I sign off and Mickey lowers the camera.

"We did it again," Dad says, beaming. "Another soul at peace."

"That's how this works?" Keaton asks. "You just pray and the door opens?"

"Haven't you seen the show?" Mickey asks.

"Not really," Keaton says, unaware that Mom is standing next to him, obviously wanting to hug him but unable to.

"My boy," she whispers.

Elsa is looking at Mickey's camera. "Does this thing see the ghosts too?" she asks.

Everyone talking at once is a bit too much for me. "Okay, let's all go," I say abruptly.

Aunt Val looks at me with concern. "Yes, you must be tired. Thank you for having us be part of this."

"Don't be rude," Mom says. "We just got here."

I want to reply, but of course I can't. Instead, I say, "Stan, you should be okay now. No more broken display cases or strange noises."

"I can't thank you enough. Moreover, Jean is finally at peace. I can't imagine being stuck as a ghost. Must be horrible."

Mom and Elsa both laugh. "It has its challenges," Mom says.

I turn my back on her and head toward the door. Everyone gets the hint and follows me outside. Unfortunately, Mom and Elsa do too. Elsa is still trying to touch the camera. She makes it move in Mickey's hand and Mickey notices the movement. She looks at me questioningly. I shake my head.

"Good night, everyone," Aunt Val says and heads for her car. Dad and Keaton follow her to the parking area. Stan retreats into the courthouse.

Mickey stays behind. "Did you see the camera just now? I swear something moved it."

"It's Elsa," I say. "She showed up. She's very interested in your camera."

"Has she been staying near you a lot?"

"She has nowhere to go and I don't think she will cross yet."

"Have you tried?"

This gives me pause. Why haven't I tried to cross Elsa? Am I selfishly keeping her here the way I am with Mom?

"I haven't had a chance," I hedge. "She wants to see her parents and her mom doesn't want to hear from me again."

Elsa pushes the camera again. "Elsa, stop that," Mickey says. "This is not a toy."

Elsa sticks out her tongue and I laugh. "She just stuck her tongue out at you."

Mickey sticks hers out, too, and we all laugh. "I need to get home. These late nights are catching up to me," she says.

I notice a darkness around her eyes. She does look tired and a little pale.

"You okay?" I ask.

Her dark eyes fly wide. "Of course. Why do you ask?" she says too quickly.

"It's nothing," I lie as we walk toward our cars. "Get some sleep," I say, giving her a goodbye hug.

"You too."

I watch her drive away before I address Mom and Elsa. "You two should not have come."

"We wanted to see you work," Mom says.

"I was bored. There's nothing to do at your house," Elsa says.

"Sorry it's boring there, but go home. I'll be right behind you." I want a few minutes to myself before going home. Normally, after a crossing, Mickey and I jam out to music. I'll have to listen to our favorite song, "Nicotine" by *Panic!* At the Disco, on my own.

Mom and Elsa disappear, and I climb into my car. I pull out my phone to play the song, and see I have a missed text.

It's from Jamie.

A possessed puppet was here.

THIRTY-TWO
JAMIE BLAKE

I can smell Graham's cologne on me, and it makes me smile. It's a cool night, but the memory of his hands on my skin keeps me warm as I make my way up the walkway to my house. A smile of contentment fills my face as I put the key into the handle and turn the lock.

"We're finally together," I think to myself as I push the door open and reach for the light switch.

My orange cat, Oscar, jumps at me with a howl and runs out the open door. Surprised, I watch him disappear into the dark.

He's never done that before.

Instantly, I'm on alert. "Hello?" I call into the house.

Something scurries across the living room and into the kitchen, startling me. I should run. I should call the police.

But maybe it's just a possum or something. Wouldn't I look foolish then? Besides, the police aren't too happy with me right now.

With my back to the hall wall, I enter the house, leaving the front door open so whatever is inside can get out. I work my way to the kitchen and turn on that light.

Then I see what's broken in and it's not a possum.

Standing on my kitchen table is a marionette. A jester with a pointed hat, blue star eyes and an oversized red mouth. It kicks mail off my table.

"What do you want?" I demand, terrified.

The strings are dancing over its head like they're being moved by an invisible hand. The thing is horrible.

It begins to laugh, its painted mouth hanging open.

"Get out!" I shout, not sure what to do, wishing I had stayed the night at Graham's the way he asked me to.

The puppet reaches a hand in my direction and hisses, "Jaaaamiiee."

"Get out!" I shout again, grabbing a broom from next to the refrigerator. I wave the broom toward the puppet, trying to knock it off the table.

It ducks away and laughs again. "See you soon, Jaaamiee," it says, then jumps off the table, runs past me, down the hall and through the open door.

I hurry after it and slam the door and turn the lock. I stand there panting, not sure what to do. What in the world was that? Will it come back? What does it want with me?

With shaking fingers, I call the only person that might understand.

Rylan doesn't answer, so I text her. *A possessed puppet was here.*

I look out the windows, but don't see it in either the front yard or the back. After a long time, I give up and lie on the couch, with my heart still racing. The phone clutched in my hand.

I mean to stay up all night, to keep vigil in case the horrible thing comes back.

I must have fallen asleep. I wake to a horrible smell and something covering my mouth. I kick against the person holding a hand to my face. I hear a crash as the side table lamp falls.

It's the last thing I hear before I fall unconscious.

THIRTY-THREE

RYLAN FLYNN

I can't drive to Jamie's fast enough. Scenarios play through my head of what Roland wants with her.

None of them are good.

I park behind her car and jump from the Caddy. I'm halfway up the walkway when I notice the front door is hanging open.

I freeze, on guard.

"Jamie?" I call toward the house. "You in there?"

I take a step, my eyes on the doorway, expecting the puppet to jump out at any moment. Another step, then another and I'm at the door.

"Jamie?" I call again. "It's Rylan. I came as soon as I got your text."

From somewhere in the neighborhood, a dog barks, a lonely sound that puts my already frayed nerves on edge.

The inside of the house is dark, and it takes all my courage to enter. I don't want Roland to surprise me, but I need to make sure Jamie is okay.

I reach along the hall for a switch and the entryway lights

up. Something crunches under my feet, broken glass. The side window is broken.

My fear level rises. "Jamie?" I call, desperate. "Where are you?"

I search the house, turning on lights as I go. The kitchen is empty, the dining room empty. The last room in the downstairs is the living room.

I flip that switch, but nothing comes on. I flip it up and down, but still no light. I take out my cell phone flashlight and shine it in the room with trepidation.

The lamp that should have come on is lying broken on the floor. A throw pillow is next to it and a cushion is pulled half off the couch.

My stomach sinks. Something happened in this room.

I turn and run upstairs, needing to find my friend and sure I won't. I search every room, calling her name.

Jamie is gone.

The house may be a crime scene, so I go out to the front yard. I take three deep breaths and the panic clears enough for rational thought.

Maybe she's with Graham.

That's probably it. She got scared by Roland and went to Graham's. That makes sense.

"I'll just call her," I mumble and dial Jamie's number. I hear a ringing inside the house.

Wherever she is, she didn't take her phone.

I hang up and call Graham. He doesn't answer. In frustration, I pace the yard. Something is terribly wrong.

I do what I always do when there's trouble.

I call Ford.

"Hey, I was just headed to your house," he answers.

"I'm not there. I think something bad has happened. Jamie texted me a while ago that the puppet was at her house. I came over here and it looks like she might have been taken. Can you come?"

"I'll be right there," is all I hear before my phone goes dead. I look at the black screen and my stomach drops.

I pace the front yard while I wait for Ford. This time of night, not many cars drive by, but each set of headlights I see makes my heart race.

"Hurry," I mumble, knowing every minute that Jamie is missing puts her in more danger. I'm sure this is connected to the previous murders and arsons.

I search the sky for the lights of a fire, praying I don't see one. It's overcast and dim, not a glimmer of fire anywhere. That's a good sign. At least for now.

My mind swirls with implications. Could it be possible that Graham is behind all this? Did he actually kill Dixie and Travis and now has done the same thing to Jamie? He didn't answer his phone. Is that because he's guilty?

I shove that thought away. Graham could not have hurt anyone.

Then who wants to hurt Graham by taking Jamie?

No matter how I turn it over in my mind, I can't figure it out. Graham is kind and gentle. Why him?

My pacing grows frantic as another car drives by that isn't Ford's.

Where is he?

I turn on my heel and Maria Weinman's ghost stands before me, her face stricken.

"Maria, what's wrong?"

"I had to find you. I just focused really hard on you and here I am."

"I don't understand, and this isn't a good time. My friend Jamie has been taken."

"I know. That's why I'm here."

"What do you mean?"

"My brother has her."

"That isn't possible. I hate to tell you, but your brother is gone. He passed away a few years ago."

"I know that. His spirit visited me before he crossed without me. My other brother, Dillon, has her."

I suddenly remember that Maria had a brother that was older. Graham barely knew him. But he's supposed to be in prison.

"Why would Dillon take Jamie?"

"To get back at Graham for what happened to me. He's been ranting about it while Jamie is tied up at the quarry in the abandoned building."

I'm hurrying to my car. "Is that where he took her?"

"He's there now, going on and on about how he wants Graham to know what loss is. I got scared and didn't know what to do. That lady doesn't deserve this and she's afraid. You're the only one I knew that might be able to help."

I throw the door to the Cadillac open and slide into the driver's seat. "I'll go there now. Go back to the quarry and keep an eye on Jamie. I'll get there as soon as I can."

"Please hurry. Dillon has gone crazy, I think. I barely recognize him."

I shut the door and start the engine. Before Maria even disappears, I back out of the driveway and speed down the street.

I pull my phone out of my pocket to call Ford and tell him what Maria said, but the phone is still dead.

"No!" I shout and throw the phone on the passenger seat.

"What's wrong, Rylan?" Elsa suddenly appears in the backseat. I'm so startled, I swerve.

"Elsa, what are you doing here?"

"Miss Margie is watching some boring show. I thought I'd

come see what you were up to. I thought you'd be home by now."

"I had to go check on my friend, Jamie."

"Is that where you're going? You're driving really fast."

"I need to go help her." I suddenly realize I'm doing it again, running into trouble without telling anyone where I'm going. I have an idea. "Elsa, you know how you can move boxes and things now?"

"I'm getting stronger every day. I even moved Mickey's camera."

"I know. You're strong. Do you think you could take a message to Ford for me?"

"I could try. What message?"

"My phone is dead and I'm in a huge hurry or I'd tell him myself. He's probably at Jamie's by now, the house I just left. Can you tell him: 'Jamie is at the quarry'?"

Elsa grows excited. "I will. I'll do it." Her enthusiasm quickly fades. "But he can't hear me."

"I know, but we have to try."

"Are you in danger?" she asks.

"Maybe. I know Jamie is and I have to save her."

"I'll do it. 'Jamie is at the quarry.' I'll remember." She disappears.

I'm alone in the car. Alone on this mission. I say a prayer that Elsa can get the message to Ford, but I don't hold out much hope. She may be able to say it, but will Ford hear?

THIRTY-FOUR

FORD PIERCE

Rylan isn't at Jamie's when I pull into the short driveway. There's no one around at all. The front door hangs open and every window in the house glows except one.

"Rylan?" I call into the house, my instincts on high alert. "Jamie?"

I enter the house carefully, my hand on my gun just in case. The living room is dark, so I shine my flashlight in and see the lamp lying on the floor next to a pillow. A cushion hangs half off the couch. There obviously was a struggle of some kind here.

But where is Rylan?

I place a call to her, but it goes directly to voicemail. I hang up, frustrated, and continue searching the house.

Neither woman is here.

As I'm coming down the stairs, footsteps stomp across the porch and through the front door.

"Jamie, are you okay?" a panicked voice shouts into the house.

Graham's worried face appears at the bottom of the steps. "Why are you here? Where's Jamie?"

"Rylan called me. She thought Jamie might have been taken," I say.

Graham leans against a wall and sinks to the floor, a piece of paper clutched in his hand. "No. I'm too late."

"Tell me what's going on," I demand.

"I got this." He holds up the paper and I take it.

A few lines are scribbled in black marker: *You took my sister, now I'll take what you love most.*

"And you think this is about Jamie?"

He sobs. "Yes. It has to be. I just found this on my kitchen table. I was in bed, but I couldn't sleep. Then I found this and came right over here. Where is she?"

"I have no idea." I read the note again, wandering into the kitchen. "Who wrote this? Is the sister Maria Weinman?"

Graham straightens and follows me. "I would imagine. I don't know who else it could be. It must be from Dillon. That's the only one who could call her sister now that Eddie is dead."

"I did a little digging on Maria today after we recovered her body. Dillon Weinman has spent the last ten years in prison for arson. He just got out last week. I was trying to track down where he is now but haven't found him yet. Then Rylan called about Jamie missing."

Graham pushes to his feet and takes the paper back from me, staring at it like it will tell him where Jamie is.

A mosquito begins buzzing in my left ear and I wave it away. "Do you have any idea where he'd take her? If he's behind the other murders, he may take her to another of your houses."

Graham shakes his head. "Those two are the only vacant houses we have. All others have new owners. You don't think he'd burn down a house with occupants in it, do you?"

"Who knows what this Dillon Weinman will do. He's obviously obsessed and hates you. I just wonder where Rylan went to. Did he take her too?"

The mosquito won't stop buzzing in my ear and I wave at it again, annoyed.

"I sure hope not. I don't know why he would."

The mosquito stops buzzing at me. "We can't just stand here speculating. Let's go under the assumption that he has them both somehow. Where would he take them?"

A sugar bowl suddenly tips over and sugar pours across the counter.

"Holy flip!" I use Rylan's pet expression. "What in the world?"

As we watch, the sugar begins to move and the letters *q-u-a-r-y* appear.

"The quarry!" we both shout at the same time.

"Thank you, whoever you are," I yell into the kitchen as we run for the front door. "Take my car," I tell Graham. We jump in and gravel shoots out from under my tires as I pull onto the road. I sit the portable blue light on my dash and turn it on. "Fasten your seatbelt," I say and hit the gas.

THIRTY-FIVE
RYLAN FLYNN

The lock on the gate at the quarry has been cut. The hanging chain makes my stomach sink. The whole drive over here I had hoped Maria was wrong. That maybe Jamie had just knocked the lamp over, then gone to the twenty-four-hour Walmart or something. A silly hope.

I leave my car on the roadside of the gate, deciding I can sneak in better on foot. I don't stop to make a plan. I just hurry down the gravel lane in the thick darkness. The sky is overcast, the moon just a faint glow behind the clouds.

As I half walk half run, Maria appears floating beside me.

"Is she still alive?" I ask the question that won't stop in my head.

"She is. Dillon has her tied to a chair and he's still ranting. Sounds like he's waiting for Graham to show up. He wants to see his face when he hurts Jamie."

"Why? Why does he hate him so much?"

"He blames Graham for my drowning, even though it was an accident. Says losing me ruined his life. He spent the last ten years in prison for arson. He burned down our family home.

Eddie told me all about it when he visited here shortly after. Well, told the water, but I could hear him."

"Sounds like a nice guy."

"Grief will make you do strange things. The really odd thing is that Dillon and I were never close when I was alive. He was years older than me and treated me like a pain in the butt, not like a beloved sister. I'm surprised he took my death so hard."

I don't know how to answer this, so I just concentrate on hurrying. Soon, we come out of the trees and reach the fork that leads either to the cliffs or to the abandoned weigh station.

"Which way?"

"He's down there in the building."

I begin running in earnest, with no idea what I plan to do once I get there. First, I need to see if Jamie is okay. Then, I need to figure out how to save her.

I wish I had waited for Ford. He would know what to do. Now I can only rely on the ghost of a little girl giving him a cryptic message.

I don't hold out much hope.

Maria and I reach the side of the abandoned building. New, it was barely more than a shack. Now, it's leaning toward the water and the roof sags dangerously. I huddle against the wall, listening. I hear a man's voice from inside, but can't quite make out the words.

"Is she still alive?" I ask Maria.

She looks through the grimy window. "She's tied up and a bit bloody, but she's alive."

A wave of relief flows over me. "I can work with that." I search the area for something to use as a weapon. The best thing I can find is a rock about the size of my fist. I lift it and test the weight.

"What are you going to do with that?" Maria asks. "He has a knife, you can't stop him with a rock."

She's right. The rock won't do much against a wild man with a blade, but it makes me feel better to hold it in my hand.

I still don't know what to do. Should I bust into the building and hit him with the rock? Should I wait and hope Ford will come? What then? What would he do?

I lean against the wall, a mix of confusion.

Then I smell the gas.

Maria peeks through the window again. "He's pouring gas all over," she shouts in a panic. "He's going to burn the building."

I don't have time for confusion and doubt. I grip the rock and make my way to the door. Before I can think too much, I kick the door down and run toward Dillon.

He spins his massive bulk and drops the can. Gas spills out on the floor, the awful smell growing stronger. In his hand, he holds a Zippo lighter open, but unlit. I don't see the knife Maria said he had.

"Rylan!" Jamie shouts as I rush into the room, the rock over my head. He's taller than me, but before I can lose my nerve, I swing with all my strength. The rock smashes into Dillon's face with a satisfying crunch.

He drops with an *umph*, leaning against the wall. His eyes drift shut behind his glasses, but open again. He focuses on something behind me.

I spin in time to see Roland leap out of a door and jump on Jamie. He wraps the strings around her neck the way he did to me. Tied to the chair, she can't fight him off.

I look from Roland to Dillon, not sure which threat to fight first. Jamie's eyes are huge and full of terror. I reach for the puppet and pull him away. This just makes the strings tighter.

"Let her go, you miserable thing," I shout, trying to untangle the strings from her neck. Roland kicks his tiny feet, then chomps his horrible mouth on my arm. I scream in pain and pull away.

Dillon is on his feet now, the knife in hand. He lunges for me.

"Dillon, no!" Maria screams. "Don't!"

Dillon freezes mid-stride. "Maria?" he asks, dumbfounded.

The room begins to glow green and Maria floats in front of him.

"It's really you?" All his attention is now on his sister. Even Roland has stopped pulling on the strings and stares at her.

I take advantage of the moment and snatch the knife from Dillon, then use it to cut Roland's strings.

He howls and grabs for the knife, but I bat him off. I grab him by the crazy jester hat and pull him off Jamie. I hold him high as he kicks and swings at me, then I toss him hard against a wall. He crumples, his cut strings lying useless next to him.

I spin to face Dillon who is on his knees begging Maria for forgiveness. I hold the knife in front of me, ready to attack if needed.

"I did all this for you," Dillon cries. "He took you from us. He ruined my life, and he killed Eddie in a way. Mom and Dad were never the same once you were gone. Maria, we loved you." He begins to cry but lifts the Zippo high in the air. His voice turns hard. "I've planned my revenge on Graham for years. I will not let you stop me."

He lights the Zippo and holds it to the puddle of gasoline on the floor.

The fumes light instantly and the room whooshes with flame. Jamie and I both scream.

"We have to get out of here," Jamie yells. "Cut me loose."

I'm already working on the ropes holding her to the chair, Dillon's knife in hand. Dillon jumps up and tries to stop me.

"I have to make him pay," he shouts.

Flames are climbing the walls, fueled by the gas. It's getting hard to breathe. I chop at the ropes a few more times, and Jamie's hands are released. Dillon tries for the knife again and I swipe at him, cutting across his chest. He steps back and I drop to my knees to reach Jamie's ankles.

Dillon jumps on my back just as I get one leg free. Jamie stands and pushes him off. I slice at the remaining tie.

It falls free.

"Let's get out of here," I scream, my skin aching from the heat of the flames.

Dillon reaches for her, but Jamie kicks him in the ribs and races for the door. I'm right behind her.

We run out into the cool of the night, Dillon close behind, Maria shouting for him to stop.

"This way!" I say and run toward the only path not blocked by trees and underbrush. The path that leads to the cliffs.

THIRTY-SIX

FORD PIERCE

I am full of doubt as we fly through the country roads toward the quarry. Did we really see a word written in spilled sugar? Is this really my life now? I debate calling for backup, but I'm not sure if anyone will believe my story about the sugar.

I finally decide to call Tyler. He's seen enough with Rylan, he'll understand. I wake him up, but he agrees to meet me at the quarry.

"You think they're really there?" Graham asks once I get off the phone. "We did see the same thing in the kitchen, right?"

"Yes. We both saw it. I don't know who it was giving us the message. Maybe Maria's ghost. If it's truly Dillon Weinman that is behind all this, taking what you love most to the place it all started does make some sort of sense. At least to a man so obsessed with revenge he'd kill Dixie and Travis just to make you look guilty of murder."

"So they died because of me?" Graham says miserably. "That's horrible."

I can't disagree.

"For now, let's focus on finding Rylan and Jamie," I say. "It's too late to save the others."

It's not until I see Rylan's car at the gate that I feel confident that she's here. Relief flows through me. If she drove here, then Dillon didn't get her. At least not yet.

The gate is unlocked, so I push it open, then drive down the lane. Rylan may have walked in, but I don't want to take the time. Through the trees, an orange glow fills the sky.

"Fire," Graham says. "Another fire."

I hit the gas and kick up gravel. We shoot out of the tree-lined lane and almost miss the turn to the office building. I pull the wheel, keeping us from sliding into the water.

The building is completely engulfed in flames. If there's anyone inside, it's too late.

I stop the car and climb out, the blue light adding to the colors in the sky.

"You don't think they're in there?" Graham asks, his voice barely above a whisper.

"I hope not," I say miserably, taking a step toward the building, but turned back by the heat. "Rylan!" I shout.

A scream echoes across the water, coming from the cliffs.

"They're up there," Graham says, running back the way we came, back to where all this began.

I follow on his heels as another scream breaks the night.

I run.

THIRTY-SEVEN

RYLAN FLYNN

Jamie and I sprint as fast as we can up the path to the cliffs, but Dillon soon catches up to us. He grabs me by the hair and pulls me against his chest. He wrestles the knife from my hand, and it flashes as he holds it to my throat.

"Stop, or I'll cut her," he tells Jamie.

She skids to a stop. "Why are you doing this?" she asks miserably. "Hurting us won't bring Maria back."

"Maybe not, but it will ruin what's left of Graham's life."

"Please, let her go, just take me," I beg. "I'm Graham's friend."

"You're the ghost hunter. I've heard all about you. I know what you do. You're the one that found my sister's body. My parents told me all about it."

"Maria led me to the bones," I say, stalling.

"Maria is dead."

"You saw her. Her spirit is still here."

"That was a hallucination," he says.

"No, Maria is here." I hope she will appear to help again, but I don't see her anywhere.

"Liar." The tip of the knife pushes against my neck.

Jamie screams. "Please don't hurt her."

"I won't hurt her, the fall will." Dillon drags me to the cliff edge. I dig my feet into the dirt, push away from the drop-off. I know that kids jump from here, that it's mostly safe.

Still, the fall killed Maria.

The knife pushes into my skin, and I feel blood dripping.

Should I jump?

A blue swirling light fills the sky to my right. I almost sink in relief.

Ford is here.

I scream as loud as I can, startling Dillon.

"Stop that."

I scream again.

Jamie takes advantage of the momentary distraction and pulls at the arm holding the knife while kicking at him. I twist out of his grip. The knife slices against the soft skin of my neck, but I manage to pull away.

Jamie is now on his back and he's swinging wildly with the knife, unable to shake her, unable to cut her.

I swipe my sneaker through the air and take his legs out from under him. With Jamie on his back, he falls to the ground. They roll around on the ground and I jump into the fray, trying to get the knife.

I see the blade and reach for it, but he moves his hand and I miss. The three of us roll and I feel my head hanging off the cliff edge. I kick and buck, trying not to fall.

A sharp pain pinches my side at the same time I hear Ford shouting. A moment later, Ford has Dillon on the ground, his knee on his back and his arm twisted behind him.

Jamie clings to Graham.

I try to sit up, but it hurts.

"He has a knife," Jamie says.

"Where is it?" Ford asks.

I reach toward the pain in my side and find the knife.

Hot blood surges onto my hands. I don't try to move, I just lie back in the dirt, my head hanging over the edge of the cliff.

I watch upside down as the orange lights of the building on fire mix with the blue from Ford's car in a beautiful dance in the sky.

It's the last thing I see before I pass out.

A lovely way to die.

My eyes slit open and a white light blinds.

Pain wracks my side.

"Stay with me. Stay with me."

I close my eyes again.

The white light returns and I float toward it.

Toward consciousness or heaven?

I lift a hand to touch my side. Even this small movement is painful.

"She's coming around." An unfamiliar female voice.

"Don't you go," Mom begs. "Don't you join me."

The light hurts my eyes, so I squeeze them shut.

It's dark. So dark it scares me.

Pain fills my body and I want to hide from it.

"Come on, Rylan. You can do it."

Ford.

Ford.

Ford.

I flutter my lids and the light above me burns.

Is this heaven? Has the door opened for me?

I squint against the glare.

It's not heaven. Just a light in a ceiling.

I blink rapidly, turn my head, and see a hospital room.

Ford sleeps with his head on my bed, my hand in his.

I squeeze with all I have, but I'm so weak I don't know if he can feel me.

He lifts his head and a huge smile beams at me.

"Hey," he says. "You're back."

I try to move, but even shifting my legs hurts. "I think so."

He kisses my hand. "We thought we were going to lose you."

"I'm too stubborn for that." I try to laugh, but it comes out more like a sob.

"Don't move. You've been stabbed and had to have surgery."

I don't want to move. I want to sleep.

"I hurt," I manage to say.

"That will fade eventually. You just rest."

I look around the room. Mom and Elsa are on the other side of my bed.

"Hey," I say to them, not caring that Ford can hear me.

"We thought we lost you," Mom says with tears in her eyes.

"You almost died," Elsa says.

I give them what I hope is a smile and then drift back to sleep.

The next few days passed in a blur of nurses giving me pain medicine that made me feel loopy and visits from everyone. Ford barely left my side. Dad prayed over me several times. Even Keaton visited with Cheryl.

Aunt Val sat with me a lot.

The entire time, Mom stayed with me. Sometimes with Elsa. Sometimes not.

When we were alone, I'd talk to her, not caring what the nurses thought about my sanity.

It didn't matter. She did most of the talking. Seems almost losing me makes her want to tell me all about her life. Some of it I know. Like how she worked here in this hospital as an ER nurse for years up until the day she died. She told me about how she and Dad met and even about how their marriage eventually fizzled out.

She talked and talked and I hung on every word, thankful for this time with her.

On the fifth day of my hospital stay, I'm sitting up in bed, eating apple sauce, when Mom appears by the side of my bed, a serious look on her face.

"I need to ask for a favor," she says, running her hand over the hole behind her ear.

I spoon the apple sauce in my mouth, swallow and say, "Anything."

"I want you to find out who murdered me."

THIRTY-EIGHT

I climb into my SUV and turn the key, thinking of work. I take a sip of my coffee and check the rearview mirror. I spit coffee onto the steering wheel in surprise.

"Hello again," the badly burned puppet hisses from the backseat.

A LETTER FROM DAWN

Dearest reader,

A huge thank you for choosing to read *The Burning Soul*. I truly appreciate you and hope you loved it. If you did enjoy it, and want to keep up to date with all my latest releases, just sign up at the following link. Your email address will never be shared and you can unsubscribe at any time.

www.secondskybooks.com/dawn-merriman

The Burning Soul was fun to write. The "thing in Keaton's room" finally escaped! What a riot to have him terrorizing Rylan from all angles. I hope you loved this book as much as I loved writing it.

If you enjoyed *The Burning Soul*, I would be very grateful if you could leave a review. Feedback from readers is so special. I'd love to hear what you think, and it makes such a difference helping new readers to discover one of my books for the first time.

I love hearing from my readers and I interact on my Fan Club on Facebook at the link below. Join the club today and get behind-the-scenes info on my works, fun games and interesting tidbits from my life.

www.facebook.com/groups/dawnmerrimannovelistfanclub

Again, thank you for reading *The Burning Soul.*

Happy reading and God bless,

Dawn Merriman

facebook.com/dawnmerrimannovelist
instagram.com/dawnmerrimannovelist

ACKNOWLEDGMENTS

As always, I want to thank "my team."

I always first want to thank my husband, Kevin. He listens tirelessly to me talking about plot and characters. It's almost like Rylan is one of our kids. His unwavering support of my career lifts me up.

To my beta reader team, Carlie Frech, Jamie Miller, Candy Wajer and Katie Hoffman, your input cannot be overstated. Thank you for taking the time to read the rough pages and offer insights.

A huge thank you to Bookouture, Second Sky, and the wonderful team there. Your continued support of Rylan means the world to me. My editor, Jack Renninson, has been an amazing guide through every book. Jack, thank you for all the time and effort you have put into *The Burning Soul*.

Thank you to my readers for choosing my stories to spend time with. That you'd choose my stories out of all the stories out there is wonderful.

Most of all, thank you to God for giving me the gift to tell the stories. I hope I do them justice.

Thank you all,

Dawn Merriman

PUBLISHING TEAM

Turning a manuscript into a book requires the efforts of many people. The publishing team at Bookouture would like to acknowledge everyone who contributed to this publication.

Audio
Alba Proko
Sinead O'Connor
Melissa Tran

Commercial
Lauren Morrissette
Hannah Richmond
Imogen Allport

Cover design
Damonza.com

Data and analysis
Mark Alder
Mohamed Bussuri

Editorial
Jack Renninson
Melissa Tran

Copyeditor
Rhian McKay

Proofreader
Catherine Lenderi

Marketing
Alex Crow
Melanie Price
Occy Carr
Cíara Rosney
Martyna Młynarska

Operations and distribution
Marina Valles
Stephanie Straub
Joe Morris

Production
Hannah Snetsinger
Mandy Kullar
Ria Clare
Nadia Michael

Publicity
Kim Nash
Noelle Holten
Jess Readett
Sarah Hardy

Rights and contracts
Peta Nightingale
Richard King
Saidah Graham

Printed in Great Britain
by Amazon

62134253R00119